D0805597

The Masterman
A North-Western Story

Other Five Star Titles by Max Brand:

Sixteen in Nome
Outlaws All: A Western Trio
The Lightning Warrior
The Wolf Strain: A Western Trio
The Stone that Shines
Men Beyond the Law: A Western Trio
Beyond the Outposts
The Fugitive's Mission: A Western Trio
In the Hills of Monterey
The Lost Valley: A Western Trio
Chinook
The Gauntlet: A Western Trio
The Survival of Juan Oro
Stolen Gold: A Western Trio
The Geraldi Trail

MAX BRAND™

The Masterman

A North-Western Story

Five Star
Unity, Maine

This novel is a work of fiction. Names, characters, places, and incidents are either the product of the author's imagination, or, if real, used fictitiously.

Five Star First Edition Western Series.
Published in 2000 in conjunction with
Golden West Literary Agency

Cover photograph by Johnny D. Boggs

Set in 11 pt. Plantin by Al Chase.

Printed in the United States on permanent paper.

Library of Congress Cataloging-in-Publication Data

Brand, Max, 1892–1944.
The masterman : a north-western story / by Max Brand.—1st ed.
p. cm.
ISBN 0-7862-2099-6 (hc : alk. paper)
1. Alaska — Fiction. I. Title.
PS3511.A87 M37 2000
813′.52—dc21 00-023527

The Masterman

A North-Western Story

Chapter One

DOG FOOD?

They came up Candy Creek when the thaw was beginning. In the middle of the day a steamy breath went up from the earth, and the brush along the banks turned brown. The central ice lifted in a broad arch, and in the gutters at the sides of the river water was pooling or running.

At a certain moment during the evening this moving water was skinned over with cold; the brush turned into black, shining glass; and the mist changed to a cloud of powdered ice. They were making good time, for the ice was smooth, and the twelve dogs, strung out in a double line in front of the sleds, were pulling heartily.

Christy, the cheechako of the party, was now hardened to his work. In learning to mush ahead at a dog-trot for hours at a time, he had left ten or twelve pounds behind him to grease the trail. He was a big fellow, and now he had the swing of it.

Although labor had cleansed his body, it could not take the evil from his mind. During the days when Jap Laforge and his little crew of mankillers had haunted the trails of Alaska, Laforge had sent his call far away. All the black blood in Christy's heart had risen to answer, and now he had put two thousand miles of the distance behind him.

It was only chance that stopped him on the way. The best time for travel was before three o'clock in the afternoon. The ice over the rounded center of the stream was less slippery going then, and the rush and music of the water in the gutters had been frozen to silence. It was then that trouble stopped the travelers like a wall. It came from the prettiest dog in the team, a silver malamute that ran in the middle of the swing. He wore a happy, laughing face all day long, but, as they rounded a bend and he was shouldered by the MacKenzie River Husky that was his partner, the malamute flashed his teeth and cut the Husky's throat with one saber stroke.

It was as though the team was one huge organism, with one body and one life. Writhing, it twisted back about the wounded place. The smell of blood automatically set all its teeth to working, and the great mound of fur began to squirm and slither down the slope toward the gutter.

These dogs had cost from seventy-five to two hundred dollars each, and the three men charged on that whirlpool of flesh with yells. Steve Christy reached it first. He had courage to match his weight. He was ashamed of the softness that he had shown at the beginning of the march, and now he charged straight in.

Expert dog-punchers can do that and hope for only minor injuries, but Christy's feet shot from under him with a force that carried him and the whole snarling maëlstrom crashing through the ice that was newly sheeted across the gutters.

Harry Allen and Polly, the half-breed, kicked, clubbed, and cursed until they had the tangle straightened out. By that time every dog was slashed, four of them were dead, and Steve Christy's right leg was torn in three places, almost to the bone. The beautiful silver malamute had seen to that.

Rapidly, clumsily, and in silence, they bandaged that leg and re-covered it with haste, for already the flesh had turned purple.

Steve Christy, having had his pipe filled and lighted, remarked: "One-third of the dogs are out, and I'll stay out with them. You can't make the trip with four dogs short, plus a cripple to pack along. Just drop me at the first road house."

Harry Allen put things clearly. He said: "We had to pull those bandages so tight that the circulation has been stopped. That leg is purple now, and it'll freeze blue in an hour or so. If it freezes, it'll have to be cut off at the hip. If it's cut off at the hip, you're a dead man."

Christy closed his eyes, opened them again. "That smoke over there," he remarked. "Doesn't that come from a cabin?"

He pointed toward a thin column of smoke that looked as though it might come from a chimney. It rose above the brush a bit before the wind cuffed it into handfuls that soon dissolved.

"That's Doc's cabin," said the half-breed, and shook his head.

"That sourdough," explained Harry Allen, "wouldn't let you in if you were the father of your country and dying on his doorstep. And it's a long march, beyond him, to the next house."

Christy leaned on one elbow and puffed at his pipe. "Those bandages are wet with blood . . . blood that will freeze. Just how bad is Doc?" he said.

"He's hell on wheels," said Allen, "and his place is full of guns."

Christy's face hardened. They had stretched him on the first sled, and now he lay back among the robes calmly. "There's one of him and two of you," said Christy, and he began to contemplate the misty night that was gathering above him.

The white man looked at the half-breed, and the face of the half-breed wrinkled as though with a grin. Then they mushed the dogs around the next bend and stopped in front of a flight of steps that were chopped out of the bank of the creek and trimmed with a straight twig set in the lip of each. These steps mounted past a canoe and a flat-bottomed boat that rested on top of the bank, each under a low housing, and above the steps a path opened through the shimmering brush.

Christy heaved himself on one elbow. His pipe was still going, and he puffed quietly at it while he watched Harry Allen take the rifle. The half-breed picked the best axe from under the tarpaulin, looked at the edge, and shook it in the ample grip of one hand.

As the pair started across the ice, Christy, with his mittened hand, took the pipe from his mouth. "Good luck," he said.

They turned, looked at him, and then went on in silence, as though they had orders to execute and each one knew his part.

Allen went up the steps first, but on the slick surface of the path above he stumbled, and the half-breed stepped past him toward the cabin. It was built of small logs, and the look of stable strength about it seemed to indicate at least a double thickness of wall, perhaps filled with a plastering of mud and moss. The chimney rose at one end. A broad shed had been built low against the other, so that the house looked like a stern-wheeler river boat, driving slowly through the Alaskan fog. Even the most secure of buildings in that wilderness is bound to appear as fragile as a ship whipping down a fierce current, with white water ahead.

Polly, the 'breed, reached the door and looked behind him, seeing that the white man had his rifle at the ready. Then he knocked. The wind that had been blowing with increasing violence stopped—or was it their own excitement that made it seem to stop?—so that they heard the hissing of cookery that went on inside the place. The starvation of the trail made them imagine that they could even smell the fragrance of hot food, each what he most desired.

Polly, with the back of the axe, knocked again. Then they

both jumped, for a dog howled suddenly in answer, close behind the door.

Polly turned his head again. The white of his eyes showed, and he was breathing hard, as though he had been running all the way from the creek.

"His dogs," he said, and swallowed.

Harry Allen seemed to feel that the remark was a little silly. He was making a fighting face himself, but he growled: "Don't be a damn' fool! Of course, he's got dogs. What's funny about that?"

There was nothing funny about it. Doc pulled the door open, at this moment, and looked out upon his visitors. Neither of his large hands held a gun; they were draped comfortably upon his hips. There was no need for guns, because he was flanked by a pair of wolfish Huskies that seemed to be leaning against invisible leashes in their eagerness to get at the strangers. A word from Doc, it was apparent, would remove any restraint. Perhaps that was the reason that a smile twisted the bearded face of Doc.

He was a tawny man, and the hair on his head and on his face had been roughed off with a pair of sheep shears, so that it looked like a thick cowl.

"Hello, boys," he said.

"Doc, we got a man down there, been mauled by the dogs," said Polly.

"Leg's all chewed up," added Allen. "It's going to freeze solid, with this wind that's blowing up." He jerked his thumb over his shoulder, and let the rifle swing down to his side.

"I'm not running a road house," said Doc. He shrugged one massive shoulder as he spoke, and reached for the edge of the door to slam it shut.

"You ain't gonna take him in?" asked the half-breed curiously.

"You *know* I won't take him in," said Doc. "And the next time fellows like you bother me, I turn the dogs loose on you. Understand?"

Harry Allen found his voice with a shout. "You're a disgrace to Alaska!" he cried. "You're not an Alaskan at all. . . . You're a mangy cur!"

Doc smiled again. "You boys have trouble enough," he said. "You don't want me to break you up, do you?"

"Listen to me!" raged Allen. "If Steve Christy dies, I'm going to let the boys at the diggings know *why* he died."

"Steve Christy?" said Doc. "Is that his name?" He swung a half-step nearer, over the threshold.

"That's his name. . . . If he dies, I'll be back here with a dozen men, and we'll show you some law that's not on the books. You hear me talk?"

"What's your name?" asked Doc.

"Allen's my name."

"Allen, you've yapped enough. How badly's this Steve Christy chewed up?"

He had asked the question of the half-breed, and Polly answered: "The dogs, they got him pretty good. They knifed him clean to the bone."

"I'll take a look," said Doc.

He strode down the path, ran lightly along the frozen steps, and stood beside the sled.

"You're Christy, are you?" he asked.

"That's my name," said the wounded man.

"Are you done in?"

Christy tapped the dottle out of his pipe. "My leg's freezing," he answered.

"Numb?"

"Yes."

"I'd better have you in, then," remarked Doc, and picked

up in his arms the two hundred pounds of Christy, plus fifteen pounds of clothes and robes.

"You boys can bring along his pack," he said, and he went up the steps and along the path to the house.

Inside, he lowered his burden on a bunk that was built against the end wall, near the fireplace. When he straightened, he was breathing deeply, but not rapidly. With an almost professional calmness of eye, Christy took note of this, but he said nothing.

"I'll feed him," said Doc. "I've got plenty of chuck here. I've got extra sleds and extra dogs, too. You boys can keep the rest of your pack, and, when he's able to travel, I'll start him along for the diggings. That's all. Now mush out of here. Get going."

Harry Allen looked toward the pots that steamed on the stove, inhaled the life-giving savors that breathed from them, and made a snarling face as he answered: "You're the boss!" Yet, with a vague and savage hope, his eyes ranged over Doc's great body. The man was big and very strong—but powder and lead are wonderful equalizers.

It was the dogs who made the difference. One of them had begun to slaver, and, when he saw this, the heart of Allen died in him. He merely leaned over Christy to say farewell, muttering at the same time: "He let you in because he seemed to know your name. I hope he doesn't use you for dog food after we're gone. So long, Steve!"

Chapter Two

DRY FOR TALK

In the Arctic, wounds close with wonderful speed, and people who live in Alaska are apt to feel that this is owing to some beneficial quality in the air. The air is pure, of course, but excellent physical condition tells the rest of the story.

Big Stephen Christy was in bed for a week only. He spent two weeks more recuperating, and would have taken the trail long before, except that his host would not permit him to leave until he was absolutely in the pink of condition.

During those three weeks, there was only one really bad hour, and that was in the beginning, when Doc thawed out that half-frozen leg with hot water. As the blood freshened on the lips of the wounds, he sewed them neatly together with a needle and fine linen thread, reaching well down into the flesh. Christy had to set his jaw a bit to endure that, but it was soon over. Then he had a vast meal of beef stew and pancakes, with a quart of powerful coffee, and fell asleep in the middle of his second cigarette, to be awakened twelve hours later.

Doc was standing over him. "I've got to make a run along my trap-line," the big, bearded man said. "That takes me two days. You won't have to move yourself about much. That stack of wood will keep you going. If you want more food than I've laid out yonder, go into the storeroom and help yourself. Will it worry you to be alone?"

Christy wouldn't mind that. As a matter of fact, the only thing that did pinch him during the two days of loneliness was an increasing hunger to find out what sort of man Doc had been when he lived in the world of men.

It seemed to Christy, from the devices that filled the cabin, that his host must have been a sailor. About the place there was a neatness and precision of arrangement that only women and sailors are apt to achieve. He noted two chairs with bottoms and backs of soft deerskin, the woodwork neatly turned; two tables, the legs fretted with a geometrical design that might have taken hundreds of hours to carve; a hanging shelf that contained a Bible, a thick almanac, a comprehensive book on trapping, a one-volume Shakespeare, and *Clarissa Harlowe* in eight volumes. Near the table was an elaborate sewing kit. There was also a stove and cooking utensils that ranged from a massive eight-gallon kettle to skewers and forks, all rather clumsily but carefully homemade.

A cupboard, framed against the wall and closed with moose or elkhide, was filled with lynx-skinned mittens, several light, warm fur suits—in particular one parka of Siberian squirrel whose hood was faced with fox and wolverine, and lined with silk!—mukluks with feet made of moosehide and tops of most delicate caribou; and great boots, homemade, like the rest of these articles of wearing apparel, and gummed to waterproof them. In fact, that cupboard contained enough clothing of various sorts for half a dozen men, through several years of Arctic life.

The bunk had a webbed bottom, and a mattress filled with down; the blankets were of rabbit skins, twisted into soft ropes, light as feathers, and then woven like cloth—the warmest bed-covering that one could imagine. The pelts of two wolves, and the skin of a huge Alaskan brown bear lay on the floor that was not merely the beaten earth, but of planks made by squaring and planing small trees.

There was a gun rack that contained a double-barreled shotgun, a pump gun, a monstrous .45 caliber rifle, a Winchester, a light carbine, and no less than four Colt revolvers. Ammunition for this armory filled a leather chest that was divided into compartments, the various kinds wrapped separately in soft leather, and labeled neatly. There was another rack filled with fishing tackle, although this was nearly all shop-made and of the finest sort, including a case that contained a large assortment of dry flies.

In the storeroom, when Christy dragged himself there to feed his curiosity still further, he found a supply of furs assorted in piles: mink, fox, lynx, wolf, rabbit (perhaps merely a reserve for the making of more robes), marten, two wolverine pelts, and several bearskins that had been cured so skillfully that they were almost as supple as felt. If these piles represented the catch of a single season, it was plain that the hermit must make a very good income from his traps.

Another section of the shed was given over to food, chiefly dried fish, frozen fish in vast quantities, frozen venison, caribou, and moose. There were also four barrels of flour, a whole sack of green coffee beans, some tinned jam, a fine bin of potatoes, and enough odds and ends of things to make a long list.

But what interested Christy more than the fur or the food stores was the blacksmith shop, that was fitted up in one end of the shed. Forge, anvil, and bellows were homemade, and along the wall hung a quantity of tools, also obviously homemade. This man had made hammers, hatchets, picks, shovels, and all the kitchen utensils. He had even wasted enough time to make half a dozen knives! Five of them were still in the rough, but one had been finished and polished and sharpened on the grindstone. The metal had a keen edge, and, although it was doubtless not up to a fine commercial cutlery, there was a good gray-blue sheen to it that promised service.

Christy looked into the charcoal bin, gave the heavy bellows a wheeze, and then worked his way back into the cabin. He was chilled to the bone. Pain was shooting through his wounds. But he was delighted with his journey.

He freshened the fire on the hearth, stuffed the stove—that furnished nine-tenths of the heat—and lay back among the downy blankets to stare at the ceiling and envy this man's wealth; for no machine-made palace could have given the same sense of luxurious comfort, or of single-handed victory over the wilderness, that this cabin conveyed.

The pressure of necessity had kept Doc's hand working until he was master of many crafts, although in years he was still nearer thirty than forty. The same pressure had formed and tempered the strength of his body until he could handle two hundred pound burdens with an easy comfort.

So through those two days, the wounded man constantly touched with eyes and fingers the achievements of the trapper; and with every contact he was flung into a tangle of imaginings, trying to reconstruct the story of Doc's past. The man's books and his speech were evidence that his trail had not started from the bottom of the heap, and it was plain that many words would be needed to cover the distance between the old life and the new.

To Christy's consuming curiosity about his host, the chief spur was what Allen had said in parting: that Steve Christy's own name had been the "open sesame" to the house of the recluse. As he looked down the days of his life, Christy was reasonably sure that whatever was known about him would not make pleasant thinking. At least not for most men. Just how much did Doc know about him, anyway?

That was why fear shrank the heart of Christy strangely,

when he heard the dog team on the home-stretch.

It grew to a wolfish babel about the house, then Doc entered in a flurry of snow, for winter had come back, after the thaw, with an icy wind and feathery showers of snowflakes trembling in it.

A bundle of furs and some clanking traps were borne in by Doc, and he stood for a moment under his load, looking about him, and nodding at Christy.

"All right?" he asked.

"All right," said Christy.

The convalescent turned on his side, and for a silent hour watched. The two Huskies came in, bristled their manes as they sniffed at the stranger, and then sat down in the coolest corner, lolling their crimson tongues, and narrowed their eyes to gleaming slits while their master filled the big kettle with water and made a fire roar about it on the hearth.

When the water was warm enough, he poured it into a shallow little tub, contrived of a tarpaulin. Then he stripped himself, and set to work with soft soap and a scrubbing brush. His neck and hands were so black that they seemed to be artificially joined to the white sheen of that body.

Christy peered with a half-admiring, half-jealous, interest at the knots that jumped in and out of Doc's great shoulders, the big fingers of strength that extended down the forearms, and the long thigh muscles that drooped in heavy furls above the knees or leaped away from them and showed the hard tendons fitting to the bone. Baths are dangerous things in a climate that makes a hoarfrost sparkle even inside a double-walled cabin, but it would have been a foolish thing to mention caution to a man so well armored. The labor on the trail had burned Christy dry, but he felt like a loose and gross hulk as he stared at Doc.

The latter rubbed himself dry, carried the tarpaulin to the

door, that he opened, and with the wind and the snow whipping his naked skin, flung the water far to the side. For an instant he looked out into the storm, then closed the door without haste, and turned back to dress. He stepped into beaded moccasins, pulled on tightly fitting trousers of deerhide, soft as velvet and white as linen.

Now that he was dressed for the house, he stewed fish in the great iron kettle for the dogs, and on the stove he started a supper of beans, soft pone, fat bacon, coffee, and huge venison steaks.

Presently, he fed the dogs outside the house, and returned to finish the steaks. Wreaths of smoke whirled to the ceiling before they were properly crusted with black and brown. Then he set the small table beside the bunk, placed one of the huge portions before his guest, and at the other table ate his own meal. After that, he shaved into the palm of his hand some plug tobacco, mixed with it shreds of well-dried inner bark of the willow, loaded his pipe, and smoked.

But it seemed to Christy that there was nothing relaxed about Doc even now—nor any suggestion of peaceful contemplation in his face. His eyes never moved slowly. Whenever a dog stirred or the fire flared, they leaped suddenly.

"Look here," said Christy. "If you prefer it this way, I won't open my mouth while I'm in your cabin. But clear to the roots of my tongue, I'm dry for talk."

The two dogs slid halfway across the room toward the speaker before their master checked them, waving them back to their corner. One slight gesture gave the command. It appeared to Christy that those big, weather-darkened hands could brush any obstacle from Doc's life with an equal ease.

"I was waiting for you to start," said Doc. His active eyes flashed to the face of Christy and steadied there, bright and sure as the glance of a marksman. He even added: "I'm too rusty to make any beginning . . . but if you'll break trail, I'll try to follow along."

"I want to ask questions . . . pounds of 'em," said Christy. "You mind that?"

"No," said Doc.

"Tell me first, then, what induced you to let me come in here? I understood that you never took in a stranger."

"You're not a stranger."

"No? Not a stranger? If I'd ever met you before, Doc, I'd remember it!"

"A friend of mine used to talk a lot about you in the old days."

"Who was that?"

"Fellow by the name of Bob Melville."

Between Christy's teeth the pipe jerked, and a thin puff of ashes hung in the air. "You mean to say that Melville had anything good to say about me?"

"I didn't say that," answered the trapper. "Melville says that you're the worst crook in the world. He wants to cut your throat. . . . So, when I heard your name, I thought that I might keep you with me until he turns up and has his chance."

Chapter Three

A LIKABLE JOB

As he listened, the cabin turned from a haven to a prison for Christy, and all at once he knew the meaning of the other man's bright, quick eyes. He had seen eyes like those before, in birds of prey and in hunting beasts.

"Bob Melville told you quite a story?" he suggested.

"The whole thing," answered Doc. "About the bank he started at Travis Junction . . . how it grew . . . how he married and had two children . . . how he took a liking to young Steve Christy and made him vice president, with a split in all the profits . . . how the hard times came . . . how the bank was robbed by a thug who knew the combination on the vault . . . how he could have learned it only from Steve Christy or Melville himself . . . how you left town, Christy, and came back with the dead body of the thug, and his signed confession that Melville had told him the numbers of the combination . . . how Melville had to dodge the sheriff after that . . . how he ran for his life and wound up here in Alaska. That's the story."

Christy considered, behind a smoke screen. "Melville left out some details," he remarked. "For instance, he might have told you that one reason he was interested in me was that I had fifty thousand dollars in spot cash to increase the capital of the bank."

"He told me that," said Doc.

"How did Melville make a friend of you?" asked Christy.

"He has a mine, back yonder. It's a good spot, where he

washes fifty pounds of dust a year. I have a trap-line, and I extend it in his direction. Naturally, he thought that I was stalking him, and he began to hunt the hunter. So we exchanged shots, after a while. . . . He missed me . . . my bullet slid through the fleshy part of his right shoulder. The light was pretty bad," explained Doc. "Melville was dead game. The slug had knocked him down, and his gun was lost in the snow. He came for me with a knife in his left hand."

Doc's face softened, and he laughed a little. "I had to rap him along the head with my revolver. That was how we came to be friends. I took care of him, here, till his shoulder was well. Now we see each other a couple of times a year."

"Since you're talking," said Christy, "what about yourself, Doc? What brought you here?"

"The same thing that brought Melville," said Doc. "A crooked friend." He said it calmly, without any accusing malice. "Cattle raising was my idea, and I went onto an American ranch, south of the border, to learn the business. The nearest American place was a little town called San Marco of the Bells, across the river, and, when I went there, I came to know a deputy federal marshal, Sandy Wiegand. We teamed together on a few parties. His job was putting down the dope traffic . . . opium, mostly, that the smugglers worked across the Río Grande and into the land of high prices.

"I was riding range, one day, when Wiegand met me and told me that he was following a trail out of bounds. He gave me a box, and asked me to ride into San Marco and hand it to a saloonkeeper called Dutch Something-or-other . . . I forget the last name. Important evidence, said Sandy, that was to be kept hidden till the right time. . . . So I took the box as far as the bridge . . . but there I was stopped, the box was opened, and a tin of opium was found inside. They jailed me for smuggling.

"I got word to Sandy, but Sandy had no answer to send me. So I got a lawyer, and, when I told him the story, he said that it would do in a book but not in a courtroom. In that part of the world a man caught in the dope traffic gets a long sentence. It seemed to me that there was nothing for it except to break jail, so that was what I did, and I swiped a horse to help me on my way.

"But in the hills a posse ran me down, and Sandy Wiegand was riding at the head of it. I killed Sandy, and that discouraged the posse so that I managed to get away. . . . That's why they wanted me in Texas for smuggling, horse stealing, and murder."

He stretched and yawned. "Time for me to turn in," he said, and rose. He took a pair of the rabbit fur robes, swept them around his body with a single twist, and lay down on the floor. One of the Huskies came to his feet, another lay at his side.

"You've told me a lot, Doc," said Christy, rising on one elbow.

"I have," said Doc. "That's what makes this a fair game. My idea is that, when you're sound, we'll give you a fair start, and then Melville and I will go after you. He has the first chance. If he misses and goes down, I take the second go at you. You'll have all the guns you want, and Melville tells me that you're quite a hand with them. . . . It'll be a strictly sporting chance."

"I am . . . quite fair with guns."

"So am I," answered Doc. "In the meantime, you and I wait here for Melville. You may be tempted to take a pass at me, but it's fair to warn you that I'm a light sleeper and that the dogs keep a close watch for me. However, as I said before, you may want to take a chance at any time. As for practice, you know where the gun rack is . . . help yourself whenever you feel like it. You'll want to know your gun before the showdown."

The lantern was on the small table beside the bunk. Christy reached for it, raised the chimney, and, stooping to blow out the flame, saw the green eyes of the wolf dogs staring at him. Afterward, in the darkness, he lay sleepless for a long time, listening to the regular breathing of his host. One of the dogs whined a little, in dreams; and from time to time the wind took the house by the shoulders and shook it, and then leaped away with a moan and a whistle. But most of the time Christy was thinking about Doc's remorseless eyes.

He drowsed and wakened again with the same problem haunting him, except that now, as a new probability, there seemed to him that there might be a chance that this was all a gigantic hoax. His reason for thinking so was that Doc had talked so freely because he took it for granted that his guest must die. Doc had confessed so much that now he would have to kill his guest. Only one thing was lacking to make that confession complete.

"Doc!" exclaimed Christy.

A quiet voice answered him at once, as though the sleeper had wakened to the instant possession of all his faculties.

"What's your real name, Doc?" asked Christy.

"Riley Oliver."

"Thanks," said Christy, and lay back again into the soft warmth of the blankets. The fact that Doc had so readily given his name convinced him that all the rest was true, that there was no hoax whatever, and that he was to be held there until he was healed sufficiently to fight for his life. Somewhere in a book he had read of such a thing—was it Robert Louis Stevenson who had told the story in which a man walked from the street into peril of his life in the house of a stranger? Christy began to mull over that question. Then, for a time, he listened to the beating of his own heart, a powerful and regular thumping, and at last he fell asleep.

He was still in bed on the fifth day, when Riley Oliver went the round of the traps again, but, before Oliver came back on the seventh, he was up and about. The leg was stiff, and he was weak, but not too weak to harness dogs to a sled and lie on it while he mushed them toward the diggings up Candy Creek, a hundred miles away. From that place he could get in touch with Jap Laforge. In the meantime, there were the guns in the rack and plenty of ammunition at hand. What was to keep him from tagging the trapper with a bullet when he drove in the dogs?

He took a rifle to the door of the cabin and sent a pair of bullets through a sapling, twenty yards away. There was no doubt that his hand was in, but, as he thoughtfully cleaned the gun and replaced it in the rack, he decided to wait. For one thing, the easy confidence with which Riley Oliver offered him this opportunity baffled him. For another, a second thaw had been arrested by a return of winter, with a heavy wind driving, day and night.

That was the last chance he had of taking Oliver by surprise, for after the second return of the trapper, there was never a moment when he turned his back on his guest, except when he left the house to tend the dogs. And if Christy strove to lock him out at such a time, the house could be burned over his head, if worse came to worst.

They maintained oddly amicable relations, like two gladiators who on a certain day in the future would have to step into the same arena and fight with swords, but who in the meantime trained together.

"I saw Melville," said Riley Oliver. "He'll be over to see you in a couple of weeks. By that time you ought to be pretty steady on your pins. Make the rounds of the trap-line with me a couple of times, and you'll be all right."

★★★★★

Three times they made those rounds, as a matter of fact, and all his strength came back to Christy. But years of training, he was sure, could never make him a match for Riley Oliver. Whether on skis, snowshoes, or simply with mukluks, the man had infinite craft of foot; and in his hands were the sleights of a stage magician. They were of a height and of an age—each exactly twenty-nine, as they discovered—but Christy knew that nothing but luck could make him the other's equal.

"This bout that's ahead of me," he said one day. "What are to be the conditions?"

"Anything you like," answered Riley Oliver. "I supposed that something like this would do. I have a dozen dogs and three sleds, all fit for racing. You take the pick of the dogs and the sleds . . . Melville takes the next best four . . . I get what's left. You have an hour's start, then Melville goes after you. I wait two more hours, and leave in my turn. First come, first served, in the matter of hunting you . . . but not two at a time. Does that sound to you?"

"That sounds to me," answered Christy dryly.

In his abrupt way, Oliver asked—the only question he had put to his guest during those three weeks—"What brought you up here to Alaska, Christy?"

"I sold out my shares in the bank," said Christy, "and I wanted a rest."

"You came up here to rest?"

"Yes. I wanted a complete change. I'm getting it," he added grimly.

That was after the third round of the traps, and the day following a hand beat twice on the door, paused, and struck again.

Oliver looked up from the scrubbing of a buckskin shirt.

"That's Melville," he said, "and he's ahead of time. Something's wrong. Or else he's been thinking red all these days, and couldn't stand it any longer." He shouted: "Come in!"

Melville entered, shutting the door carefully behind him. As he threw back his furred hood, Christy saw a face in which was a pair of deeply shadowed eyes and covered with a closely shorn black beard. Melville had been in the north for five years, but he seemed younger than at Travis Junction. His shoulders were less stooped; his stride was long and easy as he flung away the parka and walked to the fire.

"Hello, Melville," said Christy, and waited while the other looked him over with a cold curiosity.

"Hello, Christy," said Melville. The nasal twang was gone from his tone. He put his back to the fire and spread his hands to it. "You look about the same, plus a beard."

"The same to you," agreed Christy. "How are things?"

Melville had not yet spoken to the host, but now he disregarded the last question and turned to him, placing a hand on his shoulder. To Christy, it was like watching a lion tamer pat a lion.

"How are you, boy?" the visitor asked.

"Never better," said Riley Oliver.

"Are we talking in front of that?" asked Melville, swaying his head toward Christy.

"I've confided in him freely enough," said Oliver, his smile twisting his beard a little away, as usual.

"Yeah," said Melville with unmistakable sarcasm, "he's a fellow to win confidence." He turned back to Christy. "I knew you'd get up in the world, Steve, but I didn't expect to find you this far north. Somebody been finding you out?"

The imp of the perverse made Christy grin. "I'm a tired businessman on a vacation," he said.

"How much of a businessman, Steve?"

"A little over a million dollars' worth of business."

Melville regarded Christy with the calm of a long and seasoned hatred.

"When I kill you, Steve," he broke out, "I want to pull out the strings of your heart one by one . . . and unravel 'em."

Christy cleared his throat, thought better of speaking, sat down on the bunk again, and nervously clasped his knee between the interlocked fingers of his big hands. There was a pause in which the wind gripped the house and made it tremble and then ran whistling to a distance before Melville spoke.

"Is Christy fit to take the trail now?" he asked.

"Yes, perhaps." Riley Oliver, as he spoke, doused the buckskin shirt in the suds, raised it, and dipped it in clear water. Wet, the leather was a pale, bright yellow with a slimy brightness about it.

He found another small spot, and went after it with rasping knuckles. Steve Christy watched the picture of these motions with bulging eyes that saw them only faintly; he was too preoccupied with the pronouncement that he, Christy, might be ready for the trail. He knew what that meant, and, as Melville turned hungry eyes upon him, he jumped up.

"I'm not ready, Oliver . . . you know that I'm not ready! You can run three miles to my two, any day."

"He'll be able to do that as long as you live," answered Melville. "Listen to him, Riley. . . . After all, you've done for him, the cur's going to whine and beg, now."

"Wait a minute," said Oliver, with a voice half-detached from the conversation, his head still bent over his washing. "You told me that you were going to wait a while longer, Melville. You're a little early, old-timer. Christy would have been fitter for the trail if you'd waited a few more days."

"It was no choice of mine," replied Melville. "I saw the

devil, and thought it was about time for me to get into action."

"What devil?"

"Willie Birch."

At that moment Riley Oliver had been wringing out the leather shirt, but, as he heard the name of Birch, his big hands jerked with a sudden power that made the wet folds of the buckskin squeak against one another. Oliver stood up, shook out the damp roll, and gazed ruefully at the big rent that he had just made in the garment.

"Willie Birch, eh?" he repeated, laying the shirt aside.

All his preoccupation was gone now. He moved to the hearth, where he could face Melville more easily. The wavering firelight pulsed on his body, on the thick mass of his tawny beard, glittered in his eyes. It seemed miraculous to Christy that the impact of one name could have such an effect upon a man such as Riley Oliver. In the mind of Steve Christy there rose the picture of some terrible monster who strode like an ogre across the Alaska snows—Willie Birch.

"Who is Willie Birch?" he broke out at last, when it seemed that the silence would never end.

"Tell him, Bob," snapped Oliver.

"Willie Birch is the trail-man from the office of the marshal at Fairbanks," said Melville. "He's the ferret that wants to find Jap Laforge. Ever hear of the Jap?"

Then it came suddenly home to the memory of Steve Christy. The last time that Laforge, like a phantom, had appeared before him in the southland, he had spoken of Willie Birch. Year by year Birch clung to the Jap's trail. Again and again he was shaken off; again and again he returned to the task—a small man with a gigantic spirit. Yes, and other men had mentioned Willie Birch, too. He was not as well-known as Jap Laforge, of course, for he was the counter figure—the force for good that balanced against the power for evil, who was Jap. The rivalry, the hatred between the two, was building up a famous epic that would shorten hours at the campfires of the entire country.

Oliver's voice was so wonderfully gentle that Christy marveled at it. The big fellow was saying: "What happened, Bob? Come out with it, old fellow."

"I got meat-hungry, and went out to do some hunting," said Melville. "I'd gone out of the marshes and was hiking down Duck Creek when around a bend came eight dogs, running fast, and one man at the handlebars of the sled. I wanted to duck for cover . . . it's no business of mine, of course, to meet strangers . . . but the driver stopped short, and hailed me.

"I had to march up to him, and he asked me my name. He said he was Willie Birch, and that Jap Laforge was somewhere in this part of the world. He wanted to know if I'd seen him. I said that I hadn't, and I called myself Green. He fired some more questions at me. I was fool enough to say that I was trekking for the coast. He wanted to know why I didn't take Candy Creek. He had me tangled up, and I was a fool again, and tried to curse my way out of the trouble. I thought for a time that he'd pick me up merely on suspicion. But he just looked me over, and in that mind of his he printed my picture in ink that won't rub off. Then he went on.

"But I began to think it over. Birch had scared me, and, when he mentioned Laforge, I wondered, what could bring the Jap into this neck of the woods? Then my mind hit on Christy. Steve, here, is just the kind of carrion that might be a friend to Laforge. So I came over here. That's why I'm asking you if Christy is able to hit the trail. It's time for me to be finished off, one way or another."

"Pick out your outfit," Oliver said to Christy, with sudden

decision. "You know where the rifles and the revolvers are, and the ammunition. Take your choice, and then you can pick out your dogs, too. You can have your choice. You can even have Masterman, if you want him."

At the sound of his name, the larger of the two great Huskies that were Oliver's house companions slid across the floor and looked up expectantly into the face of his master.

But Christy regarded the monster without envy. He knew the murderous talents of the Masterman too well to want to have the dog in his team!

Death, felt Christy, was very close to him now. Only one ghost of hope remained. Laforge might possibly emerge from the wilderness in time to help him. However, it was folly to complain. He went grimly to pick out his weapons; in silence the others watched him, then followed outdoors to see the last of his preparations.

For one thing, Christy knew the dogs. He knew that he could not handle the pair of monsters who had slept in the cabin, but out of the rest he selected the four finest. Of the sleds, he took the lightest, newest, and strongest.

Oliver, instead of being angered by seeing so many of his possessions in the hands of a man whom he detested, seemed amused. He even said: "Melville starts one hour after you begin to mush, Christy. After Melville . . . well, I'll give you a bigger handicap. I won't start for *three* hours more. And in this sort of weather a trail may bury a lot faster than three hours."

It was true. The weather was not very cold, but a steady wind filled the whole enormous round of the sky with the gray of falling snow. The trail might be covered; that was the only hope—that or the providential coming of Laforge! But Christy, as he lashed on the snowshoes, shook his head.

Melville came up and stood over him, saying: "When I

catch up with you . . . and I'm going to overhaul you, Christy, as sure as there's a God in heaven! . . . don't think that I'll simply hail you from behind and challenge you to a fair fight. If I've any knowledge of Alaska trailing and hunting that I can use against you, I'll try it. You're not a real man to me, Christy. You're only a beast that's managed to eat five years out of the heart of my life. For every minute that you've managed to keep me away from my wife and children, I'll get something back from you."

Melville was a big fellow, but Christy, in rising, loomed formidably above him.

"D'you think that I worry about you?" he said. "I stepped on your face in the old days, and I made my fortune. I could step on your neck today . . . and break it for you. It's only that inhuman devil back there that I'm afraid of," he added, nodding his head in Oliver's direction.

He turned suddenly, called to the dogs, and the four of them lined out instantly, straight and true.

Melville watched them out of sight, and then turned back to big Riley Oliver, concern in his face.

"It's going to be a job," he said. "He's been with you on the trail too many times, and he's learned too many of your tricks."

Oliver laid a hand on the shoulder of his friend, saying: "I know how you feel with a stern chase ahead of you, but let me tell you that there's something in my bones that tells me that one of us will have the killing of him, sooner or later. And it's a job that appeals to my sweet-tooth, Bob!"

Chapter Four

AN UNCONQUERED CAPTIVE

Steve Christy, as he fled, looked the truth fairly in the face, saw his only chance, and determined to take it. Bob Melville, hardened and strong from five years in the Arctic, would make a formidable opponent, but he must be met and handled. He must be left dead on the trail, and his four dogs incorporated with the team that Christy was using, and then, with that team of eight, Christy would have to try to outfoot big Riley Oliver. That was the only possible manner of escape, he was sure. For although he was a good man with his hands and an excellent shot, he possessed a vast certainty that he would not stand for a moment against Oliver.

According to this plan, speed did not greatly matter in the beginning. It was better to save himself and his dogs for the work that would come later on in the day. So he slanted through the woods until he reached Candy Creek. The sharp banks of the little stream gathered the wind like a crooked funnel in which the blowing mists of snow whirled into vague, towering forms, or scurried swift and low, like running dogs.

Christy found an easy slope and ran the sled down to the face of the creek. There it was bad going, for in places the snow was lodged in heavy drifts, and again the wind had worked the ice smooth. He had to halt to pull off the snowshoes, lash them to the pack on the sled, and strike out in mukluks. As he struggled, sometimes with a wide vision both before and after him, sometimes choked and blinded by a sudden flurry of snow driving on the wind, he envisioned

Riley Oliver striding with the ease of a giant over both rough and smooth. Oliver's lead dog, which he had called Masterman, would find a way to hurl the sled through the snowdrifts as though through puffs of feathers. Well, eight dogs are better than four, even if there is a Masterman among the quartet; so everything depended on the chance of capturing that team of Melville's.

Christy was brooding on those chances when a burst of wind fairly stopped him in his tracks, winnowing the very flesh from his bones, and letting the cold strike into his marrow. As that squall eased, the dogs set up a clamor, and from the right hand bank, sloping down it at dizzy speed, ran a team of eight Huskies, a single long, narrow Indian sled behind that came whipping out onto the ice of Candy Creek.

A lone man was at the gee-pole. Melville? No, surely there had not been sufficient time for Melville to come up; besides, this was a little fellow.

He halted his team when it diagonaled across the way of Christy's gray leader, tall and shaggy as a timber wolf, and the driver came back to Christy with his left hand raised in salute.

It was good to see him, even though he was small. It would have been good to see even the wildest Indian, considering the sort of company that was coming up the trail behind.

There was a moment of ease in the weight of the storm, and the stranger threw back his hood to show Christy a lean face that came to a point in the tip of the nose while all the other features drew back, above and below. There were bright little eyes, and a hard iron wedge of a chin. He walked with his head canted forward. He looked as though he might be capable of fighting with his teeth.

"I am Willie Birch," said the stranger. "Who are you?"

"You're Willie Birch?" shouted Christy. He remembered the awe which that name had spread in Oliver's cabin, and he shouted still more happily: "I'll tell you who I am. I'm the man in the world that's happiest to see you. My name's Steve Christy!"

He held out his hand. It was true that this was the ferret who had been hunting Jap Laforge for years, but that made no difference to Christy at the moment. What he saw was a deep haven of refuge in a time of need.

The trail-man from the marshal's office at Fairbanks took the proffered hand in a grip that was not exactly enthusiastic. "Nobody's glad to see me, except when he's in trouble. What's the matter with you? What's eating you?"

"A pair of the good citizens that you leave loose on the trails up here . . . a bank robber and a murderer who are hoofing it after me. If you're making a collection of thugs for your jail in Fairbanks, they'll make a beautiful couple of specimens!"

At this jauntiness of speech Willie Birch frowned. But Christy went on: "You met one of them this same day . . . the fellow who told you he was trekking for the coast. He's the Montana bank robber!"

"Most of the time I'm a fool," said the trail-man, with astonishing frankness. "Now, suppose you tell me what you know."

Eloquently but swiftly Christy told his story.

"So that's the yarn behind Doc, is it?" commented Willie Birch. "Yeah, he's worth collecting. This fellow Melville we'll pick up in the course of the day's work, but Doc Oliver . . . or Riley Oliver . . . if that's his name, is going to be worth taking in."

"You won't take him in," warned Christy. "Mind you, Birch, I know that you're a good man with a gun. I can shoot a little myself. But we'll never put hands on Riley Oliver till he is dead."

A faint smile worked at Willie Birch's face, making it more ferret-like than ever. "I've seen 'em before . . . these hard gents that can't be had alive. But outside of Jap Laforge. . . ." His voice trailed off, and his eyes wandered hungrily toward the great ambition of his life.

Christy was worried. No matter how self-confident Willie Birch was, no matter what his fame, it would be strange, indeed, if he could take big Riley Oliver alive.

The trap which Birch laid for Melville was exceedingly simple. His own dog team and that of Christy were cached well in from the bank, in the brush, while the two men went downstream to a sharp bend of Candy Creek. On one side of the curve Christy waited; on the other, at the top of the bank, lay Willie Birch.

Then Christy cradled his rifle in his arms and steadied himself to patience. He felt the wind slacken, saw the spume of flying snow thin away to a grayness that the eye could penetrate easily, like a thin mist of rain. It was not long after this that he heard a voice roll echoing over the ice, and saw the dog team rounding the turn with Melville at the gee-pole, running well. There was a sharp quiver of satisfaction in Christy's heart as he stepped from the rôle of hunted into that of hunter. He rose, made a stride clear of the brush along the bank, and leveled his rifle with a shout.

He had a clear advantage as he steadied his sights for a bull's-eye in the center of Melville's body, but Melville was not ready to make an easy surrender. He reached back, plucked his own rifle from the pack on the sled, and certainly would have fired had not Willie Birch's cry rung in his ears at that moment.

Christy's finger was curling eagerly around the trigger of his rifle when he heard the same cry, with its formidable ending—". . . in the name of the law!"

Perhaps it was that phrase, even more than the certain knowledge that he was being taken in front and rear at the same time, which made Melville pause. He stood rigid. A flurry of snow half obscured him, then cleared away, and showed him in the same position, with a rifle at the ready. Had there been a bayonet in the gun, he might have posed as a Russian grenadier, standing ready to receive a charge.

Willie Birch walked straight up to his quarry and slapped him boldly on the shoulder.

"I'm Willie Birch from Fairbanks . . . the marshal's office . . . and I want you for bank robbery," he declared. "Put down that gun."

To the amazement of Christy, who still kept his bead steadily drawn, Melville actually obeyed. It seemed miraculous that a man so desperate and so determined should submit in this way; it took Christy's breath and sent through him a queer tang of fear.

Then he walked out and confronted a helpless prisoner whose hands were secured by a pair of bright little steel cuffs, with a length of chain between them.

"You see what comes of trying to pile murder on top of robbery, Bob Melville?" demanded Christy. "You see what . . . ?"

"Let him alone!" commanded Willie Birch. "The judge and the jury can decide what sort of trouble is ahead of him. That's a fine string of dogs!" He went to look them over in detail.

Melville, all this while, had stared with wide, hypnotized eyes at Christy. Now he spoke slowly: "God help the pair of you. Riley will be coming up, before long, and I say again . . . God help the pair of you."

"We trapped you, and we'll trap him the same way," answered Christy. He came close and sneered down into Melville's face. "I always had luck to beat you before . . . luck and brains. Now I have the law on my side, too."

Melville looked back with a curious calm, as though he was staring at a picture painted on a wall, rather than at a living face. There was no anger in his voice as he answered: "You're a dead man, Steve. You're as dead as though the worms were already in you. You can have the luck and the law on me . . . but Riley Oliver's coming, and he is too big for the touch of things like you."

Chapter Five

A DEMAND FOR BATTLE

Between Melville's departure and his own there were three hours for Riley Oliver to spend, but he spent every moment of them in busy preparation for the trail. The harness was in good condition, and so was the sled, but he went over every inch of each. He went over the feet of the dogs, too, and, although they were sound, he added to his load—which was chiefly fish for the team—a number of sets of moccasins in case the trail proved to be unduly prolonged and they struck a going of rough, broken ice.

Then he tried his hand with rifle and revolver—particularly with the latter, since he had had enough rifle practice in the ordinary course of his work to keep him in good form. He took bits of wood, threw them high over his shoulder, wheeled, and shot them out of the air. Only two out of six he missed completely. These failures made him shake his head.

Whatever he did, his big leader, the Masterman, observed with an intense interest. The rest of the dogs sufficiently feared their owner, but Masterman loved him with a hungry devotion. "Hungry" was the only word, for sooner or later the trail of Riley Oliver generally led to some sort of exciting trouble, and for Masterman trouble was better food than frozen fish. He was a rare fellow, the Masterman. He could use his saber-shaped fangs to hamstring a moose or to open a tin of beef without cutting his lips. He knew the voice and step and scent of everything that stirred in the white north. He had run wild with a wolf pack for two years, and, although his immense size showed that he was not pure timber wolf, he had the brains and cunning of the untamed.

It had cost Oliver two years to train Masterman, but now he was as efficient as a repeating rifle with a hair-trigger—a repeating rifle in skillful hands. He was a loose leader—a name which is often used but rarely justified, for a loose leader is really a dog that will range ahead of the team and find the buried trail, even nosing and scratching for it a foot beneath the surface if necessary. A loose leader will read the mind of treacherous ice. He knows where the team must be turned away from the face of the river. He knows where the dogs may draw the sled, if they take it at a dead run. He knows rotten ice as well as he knows rotten wood. He serves the dog-puncher, in fact, as a sort of extra intelligence, working in advance. In addition, he may be put back into harness to help the rest of the team lug through bad ground; and once in harness, he must bring out of his fellows double their usual efforts.

The Masterman could do all of these things, but his real pleasure was not so much in demonstrating his superiority over other dogs as in proving himself a worthy companion of his master when the latter went hunting. That was when they worked together like two eyes in one head. The man contributed the gun and the infinite dexterity of a man's hand; the dog offered to the partnership a courage as keen and as deadly as a hurled spear, besides all the infinite lore that is learned through the ear, and, above all, through the nose. It made a perfect combination. They fitted one another as the blade fits to the handle of a knife—as the bullet fits the gun barrel.

Now, the three hours being ended, they started out at Oliver's shout, and the Masterman knew that a hunt was on—a hunt of such a nature as he never had taken part in before. He had gone on the trail with Riley Oliver after anything from rabbits to bear or moose. But now, it was plain, another game was on foot, a game that was no less than the hunt for a man.

So a tremor ran through Masterman's mighty body. The hair lifted along his back, and he whined with a savage joy.

Presently they came out of the woods, down the steep side of Candy Creek, and out onto the ice. For a mile they continued to run, but, when it was apparent to Riley Oliver that the flight was to be made straight up the ice, he halted the team, stripped Masterman of harness, and turned him free to run well in the lead, like a telescopic set of eyes and ears—an advance intelligence.

Far off on the straight-aways, pausing again at the bends to let the team come closer, the Masterman acted as the advance guard. Now he ranged to this side, now to that side of the stream; now he ran up the bank and stood for a moment with his quarters squatted, his nose pointed up into the wind while he read with closed eyes all the signs that blew down the gale.

Under that cover, as confident as though a thousand armed men had been marching before him, Riley Oliver kept on his way. He had only three dogs, but for the time being they could make as much speed as he required.

Since the wind had fallen greatly, it was possible to look well ahead. He heard Masterman give that short, high-pitched howl that plainly meant "Danger!" On the heels of it, a rifle report rang out surprisingly flat and small through the gray air, and Riley Oliver saw Masterman fleeing away from the next bend of the banks of the stream.

A man stepped into view, firing repeatedly at the fugitive; but as a snipe flies, with ragged jerks down the wind, or as lightning jags across the sky, so the great wolf dog dissolved himself into a dodging streak of speed that brought him suddenly into the safety of the brush that at one point grew low down on the side of the bank.

The marksman, at the same time, disappeared around the bend of Candy Creek just as Oliver raised his own rifle for a shot.

Straightway, Oliver turned his team to the side of the ice, ran the sled lurching up the slope, and halted in a thicket of the small, winter-blackened trees. There he left the three sled dogs and turned to Masterman, who had come back to him and now stood before his owner with a bristling mane and eyes that were two green rays of light.

Another man would have trembled for his skin, but Riley Oliver understood that the dog was asking for battle. Somewhere in the lead were enemies that the dog wanted to strike at. Masterman, with the wisdom of all the wild, knew that man alone may stand against man, and so he waited there for Oliver to follow on the trail.

Who were those enemies? There could be no explanation for the attack upon the dog just now, except that Christy was there. Yet it was not Christy who had stood out to fire at Masterman. In spite of the distance, and with an eye long-practiced in range-finding, Riley Oliver knew that the man with the gun had been a comparatively small fellow. What, then, had become of Melville?

Out on the ice was the sign of Melville's sled and his team, together with that of Christy. Had he reached some snag, poor Melville, in the rounding of that point of land? The face of his friend was drawn again in the mind of Riley Oliver, the features rugged and stern almost to savagery, but capable of being changed by a smile. There was a wild gallantry in Melville. On that day when Oliver had first met Melville, Oliver's bullet had knocked him down. Yet Melville had risen again and come fiercely in, with a knife to take the place of his fallen gun. The length of a Colt's barrel laid well along the head had to be used to put him out of the battle.

If he had met enemies, yonder, probably he had fought to the death. Probably he was now lying with his face turned up to the senseless sky, while Christy and that other, that smaller man, whoever he was, spread the snare that the Masterman had revealed to Oliver.

This was the thought of Riley Oliver as he slung the rifle on his back and took out his revolver—for if there was fighting in these woods, it was apt to be at close hand. Then he waved to the wolf dog, and that eager monster instantly was away, skulking like a soundless shadow, testing the snow with his broad pads before he let his weight come down.

Presently before the dog a patch of snow seemed to come to life and blow away. It was a snowshoe rabbit, skidding away with incredible speed; but the Masterman was not tempted to leave his stalking. What he wished to feed was not his belly, but an infinitely nobler and more terrible appetite.

Behind him came Riley Oliver, again secured by his advance guard of Masterman's keen eyes and those trembling nostrils that could read secrets that were guarded by walls of wood or of stone. Moving steadily on, the pair made not a whisper in passing over the brittle snow and over frozen twigs that were ready to snap with pistol-shot loudness.

They came to a spot that more men than one would remember. Swelling out of the ground with enormous, wide-spread roots, was the stump of a tree that deserved to have stood in some southern region of heavy rains and rich, deep soil. By some freak of chance or location, it had found rootage here. Between the side of that stump and some brush that looked like a devilish entanglement of iron wire, the Masterman paused and sank to his belly, then twitched his head half around to warn Riley Oliver with a glance.

The glance was not needed; the movement had been enough to make Oliver raise his revolver, feeling the trigger delicately through the softness of his lynx-skin mittens.

A shadow stirred behind the brush; the head and shoulders of a man rose—Steve Christy! And another, smaller shape beside him. They were not lying in wait; they had been working their way to stalk Riley Oliver. All in an instant, the three men sighted one another.

"Go in!" yelled Oliver to the dog, and fired straight at Christy's head.

The big fellow pulled the trigger of his rifle in response, but it was a mere instinctive action. The bullet flew wild, crackling among the branches of the trees, while Christy flung up his hands and fell sidelong to the ground.

The smaller man at Christy's side had been far swifter in getting his rifle into action, but, as he jerked the butt into the hollow of his shoulder to fire at Oliver, another danger struck up at him from the ground. It was the Masterman, who at Oliver's command had launched himself as if from springs. Shooting in low, he leaped for the throat of little Willie Birch. The latter had only time to strike blindly with the butt and lock of his gun at that flying danger, and the blow diverted the teeth of Masterman only by inches from their mark. Instead, they caught Birch's fur parka, ripped it as though with a knife, and hurled Willie Birch head over heels into the snow.

His fall was like that of a cat. Birch came up to his knees with his rifle gone, but with the long blade of a hunting knife curving down brightly from his hand. The Masterman had whirled to finish his kill, but he leaped sidewise from the threat of that sharp steel, for well he knew what men can accomplish with a single fang such as that, luminous as an icicle when the first frosts begin.

The wolf dog whirled to take his enemy from behind, but Oliver's voice stopped him, thrust him tensely back on his haunches, slavering with eagerness, trembling with battle-lust.

Riley Oliver, in the meantime, gave one glance at the prostrate body of Christy, half lost in the snow and in the entanglement of the brush. That glance seemed to tell him enough, for he saw the stain of red where blood flowed from the head of Christy into the snow.

There remained only the smaller fellow with the pointed, weasel-like face, and Oliver covered Birch with his revolver as he stepped in and halted the attack of the dog. He saw the bright ferret eyes measure him, linger for a yearning instant on the steadiness of the leveled revolver. Then Willie Birch obediently dropped his knife and stood up.

"Put up your hands," commanded Oliver.

"Damn you," whispered Birch, choked with shame and fury.

"Leave 'em down for a minute then, if it eats you so close to the bone. Which of you killed Bob Melville?"

"Melville?" asked Birch. "He's not dead."

"Not quite, eh?" As he asked the question, the tawny mask of beard twisted a little to the side.

"He hasn't even been touched."

"Where is he, then?"

"Tied, back down, on my sled."

The shock of surprise brought a grunt from Riley Oliver. "That sounds like a lie to me," he said.

The little man made no answer. With his undaunted eyes he kept probing at Oliver's big body.

"He gave up without a fight. Is that what you mean?" asked Oliver harshly.

"We had him covered in front and behind. He gave up."

"You're a partner of Christy's, are you?"

"I worked with him."

"You've worked your last day, then," said Riley Oliver savagely. "If he's a rat, then you're a rat, too . . . and a rat I know him to be. What's your name?"

"Willie Birch."

The reply was sullen.

Riley Oliver scanned his prisoner again, from the bright, steady eyes as far as the torn parka and the bleeding shoulder. He remembered Melville's encounter earlier in this same eventful day.

"Your shoulder needs fixing," said Oliver.

He tore out the sleeve of Birch's shirt and with it worked a tight bandage over the wound, where the teeth of the Masterman had torn the upper arm and shoulder of the man of the law.

"If you're Willie Birch," said Oliver, "you'll start hounding my trail as soon as your arm is in shape for another fight. But I can't help that. I'll turn you loose as soon as I've made sure of my friend Melville. In the meantime, just wait here till I've brought up my team. I hate to make sure that you won't run, but I'll have to tie you, Birch."

He took a thin, supple rawhide thong from an inner pocket. With that he secured Birch's wrists behind his back and around a narrow tree. As he got in the last knot, it seemed to Oliver that he heard a faint sigh near him. He turned suddenly toward the place where Christy lay, but the man was motionless. The red spot on the snow seemed to have enlarged a little, however.

Riley Oliver went back to the spot where he had cached his team and brought it up without haste, for the dogs had heavy work through the rough snow that lay under the trees—and certainly the picture he had left behind him would not be troubled by the touch of any stranger's hand in his absence.

Yet, when he came back to the great stump, his mind reeled as he saw that Willie Birch was no longer bound to the tree.

Oliver ran past the dark tangle of brush. In the place where Christy had lain, there was only the empty imprint left by his body, and a blood reddened spot where the head had been.

The shot must have glanced. There was no other explanation. Christy had fallen, stunned, and the sigh that Riley Oliver thought he had heard could have been nothing but the first deep breath drawn by the returning consciousness of the wounded man. Afterward, he must have roused himself, then freed Willie Birch, and the two had gone together. Where?

Oliver waved Masterman ahead, to range once more as advance guard, and the sled slithered and jumped and bucked like a living thing as the dogs yanked it over the hummocky snow. The trees moved past slowly, then in a rapid stream. Oliver brought the gait to a hard run, and they broke from the trees into the last clearing near the edge of the bank, the place where many men and dogs had been trampling about.

That held the attention of neither Oliver nor the Masterman. The great dog stood on the steep bank of Candy Creek and stared straight up the course of the stream. More than half a mile away, two outfits were rapidly retreating—two outfits of eight dogs each, one team pulling a pair of small sleds, and one hitched to a long toboggan of the Indian type.

The whirling snow-mist allowed Riley Oliver to see the picture for a moment only, then blotted it with gray, and dissolved it utterly. Still gripping the gee-pole of his sled, he stared before him, thinking of the terrible labor that was to come. Two eight-dog teams to break trail for one another—two men, two brains to work at every problem—aye, and they would force Melville to help.

So Riley Oliver stared and was daunted. Although his heart shrank, there was never a doubt in him that he would strive with all his might to overtake them before they reached the diggings at the head of Candy Creek.

Chapter Six

A LOST RACE

The two men were wounded. That was Oliver's chief consolation as he mushed the team up the ice of Candy Creek against the wind, with Masterman once more back in harness. Birch's torn shoulder and arm were sure to grow inflamed, and the bullet that had grazed Steve Christy's head probably sapped some of his self-confidence, at least. Therefore, it seemed highly improbable that they would want to turn back and fight.

If he pressed them too hard, would they kill Melville rather than see his rescue? Christy was capable of that, to be sure. But in the bright, dangerous eyes of little Willie Birch there had been nothing but honesty, and an honest man of the law does not murder his prisoner. Even with one arm helpless, Birch would probably retain his command of the party and prevent Christy from following his own brutal desires.

The race was to the swift, therefore, and Oliver could afford to burn himself up in one consummate effort. Melville naturally would obstruct them as much as possible. Christy was by no means a champion musher, and of the three, only little Willie Birch was a famous traveler. Hence, Oliver made his challenge right at the beginning of the race, running twenty-four hours without stop.

With every pause he talked and sang to the four dogs. To the sled dog, powerful, patient, with no thought except to pull with all his might, he spoke in one way; to the nervous swing dog in another; and to Masterman he spoke in no tone at all, but simply thought aloud, knowing that the great leader would understand.

Singing helps soldiers on a march; it also helps racing dogs as they strain up the white monotony of a trail. The sleds whipped lightly and rapidly along, with the master running at the gee-pole, giving the dogs his cheerful voice whenever the pace slackened and his breath returned to him. He whistled the old tunes; he sang to his team the songs with which he had driven cattle along the trails in other days, or with which he had quieted them when they were bedded down by thousands in the darkness, and the night guard circled them, crooning melodies.

He watched his team throughout that day, as a prize fighter watches his own strength waning in a long fight. For twenty-four hours he struggled without catching the fugitives. His team began to fail—except the Masterman, who could borrow strength from the devil. And then the sign he followed left the creek and turned toward the southeast. He could guess what that meant. They had seen him coming—they had seen him gaining—and at last, fairly run off their feet in spite of their sixteen dogs, they had left the smooth creek and had taken to the rough going.

He followed. They were pointing straight toward Fairbanks—on the other side of the mountain range.

Half an hour later he glimpsed the dark procession that wound swiftly before him, but he could not gain upon it. Gradually, they drew away, for across the rotten, patchy ice of the open country the superiority of their dog-power told. So Riley Oliver made camp and slept that session out with twitching nerves and jumping muscles.

Two days later the mountains were heaped about them in enormous, frozen waves. Snaky mists crawled through the valleys, but the upper summits were always a sheen of ice and snow. The cold grew terrible, more penetrating than heat, and it was driven by a constant wind. Even their dense coats and the heat of labor could not keep the dogs from trembling. It seemed to the man that his body was clad in nakedness day and night.

There was no trail now—no shadow of a way. The pass he struggled through was littered with boulders varnished with ice; furthermore, the ice and snow slipped from the impending heights, and time after time blocked the way with great masses. Often he had to pack the load on the backs of the dogs, and, taking it forward, he would return with the Masterman to bring up the sled. For the big dog knew how to help—bracing his feet on a narrow ledge and gripping a sled-runner with his teeth, he understood how to haul back.

These moments of necessary relay work burned up Oliver's very soul with impatience, for there were three pairs of hands to work in the outfit that he was trailing. Three pairs of hands, and three clever brains.

Finally they reached the height of the pass, and started the descent. That was far harder than the climb, for as a rule the way was slippery as glass. The wind, roaring and bucketing through those icy ravines, struck man and beast with sudden blows from unexpected quarters.

Hardly an hour beyond that summit, a wild, rushing torrent of air sent the big yellow-coated number two dog staggering to the brink of a precipice. He wavered there, clawing desperately, weighted down by the heavy pack he carried, and still buffeted by the savage attack of the gale.

Oliver came up on the run, half a second too late. As the dog went down, his master dropped on hands and knees to peer over the brink. He could see nothing of the end of the Husky, for a hundred feet beneath them flowed a tumbling torrent of white fog. Through that the dog had fallen to a distant death.

With the team weakened by this loss, he was burdened again by the necessity of fitting moccasins to the feet of all the dogs. Even Masterman, whose pads ordinarily seemed to be of hard-woven steel threads, now limped as the razor-sharp fringes of the ice clipped through the skin to the bone. Twelve feet had to be clad in leather that was frayed out or slashed to bits in a single day's march, perhaps. He had brought plenty of leather for the purpose, and he made new moccasins during the halts.

But it was the tying of the shoes to the feet of the dogs that took the time. It was work that had to be done with care, if the moccasins were not to be stripped off after a few steps.

Three days they struggled through that glassy hell on the downward journey, and far below, through rifts in the clouds, he had occasional glimpses of the dark lowlands and the smoky woods beneath.

Then, in the course of a three-hour march, they came out of the stony heart of winter, out of the rigorous breath of the storm winds and into spring weather. From white rock, the snow turned to brittle sponge, every pore of it filled with water. The ice casing of the rocks was worn away into holes and patterns, and in some places the sheet was sprung clear of the stone and cast upon it the filmy shadows of its transparency. Everywhere was the sound of running water. It boomed in the cañons; it mourned far away; it bubbled and sang underfoot. In the sun there was warmth that made the dogs loll their tongues, while their master stripped off his furs. Soft winds were sluicing through the cañons. Beyond a doubt, the thaw was on, and the rest of the way to Fairbanks would be slushy going—the worst of the year.

In big Riley Oliver's heart there was no rejoicing because of the coming of spring. He saw in the thaw only another obstacle interposed between him and the goal that was before him. His nostrils flared, and he cursed as he worked the dogs down the slopes to the lowlands beyond.

That night might bring a freeze, and, if so, he could make good time. There were still many scores of miles between him and Fairbanks, and many-handed as the enemy were, and strong in dogs, they might yet be overtaken. But if it meant packing in the rest of the way—well, they were three, and he was only one. They were three, even though one of them represented forced labor.

Still, as he pitched camp, he waited for the warm wind to stop blowing, and bitterly he noted that his naked hands and face were not stung by the waspish frost that was usually abroad in the night air. He slept with unpleasant dreams during four hours, and then awakened to sit up with a start, as though some enemy were leaning above him.

It was the same wind, even warmer than when the sun had been shining through it. And it seemed to him that the hushing noise of the thaw was whispering to him from far away, to announce that the country would be a soggy white slough by the following morning.

He slid out of the sleeping bag where he had been stifling, and began his preparations for the last stage of the march. The sled would be abandoned here, and the dogs would pack the necessary food the rest of the way.

He estimated the distance, measured the labor, credited himself with luck, and the dogs with ability to run one full day on empty bellies. Then he arranged the packs. They were very light, considering what still had to be done. He abandoned the little primus stove. A stew kettle would do for the dogs, and, for himself, a bit of flour and water and salt, toasted on the ends of sticks, and a bit of bacon cooked in the same way. As far as that went, he could live almost on fat, during the remaining days of the journey.

It might be that the others were already nearing Fairbanks, for it seemed to him that he had been literally crawling and idling on the way. But the next morning, before he had been going two hours, he struck their sign. It could be no one else—there were three men, and a great string of dogs. They had passed there the day before, perhaps—before the thaw really put its fingers down into the snow, turning it to slush—for the sled-runners had not cut down very far into the snow.

Only one day ahead of him! He could swear to that, and he promised himself to overtake them on the way. If only their march with the sleds had not been too great—if only they became bogged down soon enough in this same white mud that was hampering him.

But all that day, as he strained forward, the marks of the runners remained, rotting deeper and deeper in the snow, to guide him. Yes, they had gained a priceless distance before the thaw held them up.

That day, and half the next, the sign of the sleds remained on the snow. But then he came to a place where it was obvious that the packs had been transferred from the sleds to the dogs and to the shoulders of the men. Only the empty sleds, probably, were being hauled along now, and there was a whole heap of abandoned litter at the point of the change, which rejoiced him savagely. It was as though he were putting his teeth into his work for the first time.

The wind helped, covering the earth with mist, reaching its warmth deeper and deeper into the snow. In the evening it began to rain. There was no shelter for either him or the dogs; there was not a bush or a tree anywhere in this waste. So he slogged on through the darkness into the faint dawn and the misty day once more, before he found a camping place. He was badly spent, and so were the dogs. Still the sign of the trail led him on. It seemed to have been made long before, although the effect of the rain made it difficult to judge the number of hours.

So, day after day, he punished himself, till the ache in the small of his back was continual, and his knees bowed and sagged as he walked. The dogs were failing rapidly, too—except Masterman. The devil that lived in that monster sustained him now. Red-eyed, he drove the staggering Huskies before him with many a shrewd nip and warning snarl, or else leaned his weight against a long leash, the end of which was clasped by Oliver, who was helped forward like a child on a leading string.

They came to rolling country, with trees scattered across it, and reached the Tanana River. It had not broken up, although the ice was drifting with loud groans and rumblings. They crossed the river and drove straight on for Fairbanks. Despair was darkening Oliver's mind, for not many miles remained. He was clinging to his purpose with a grip that was automatically locked, like the teeth of a bulldog.

Then, in the afternoon of the same day, he saw the goal before him—the string of dogs, and three men working them forward through the milk-white mist.

Oliver's lips parted in a cry. A warmth of savage triumph made him young and strong as though he had but begun the trail, and even the wind that struck him from behind, scattering the mists, seemed to him at last a favoring sign from nature. A moment more, and it had rolled back and scattered the fog so thoroughly that he saw a dark outline ahead of the quarry he was striving for. It grew clearer; it developed out of obscure distance; and now he saw that it was the town of Fairbanks itself. The three men ahead of him were on the very point of entering the place, and he had made his mighty march in vain.

Chapter Seven

A MIRROR TO THE PAST

The strength went out of him like light from a lantern struck by the wind. He dropped to one knee, while the gasping, staggering dogs gathered about and stared at him, red-eyed with exhaustion. Only Masterman stood as ever, with arched back and sharply pricking ears.

Even thought now moved with a sluggish current in Oliver's mind. But one thing was all too clear—that Melville was in for robbery only, whereas if Riley Oliver were picked up, it would be for murder. Nevertheless, from the first, there was never a doubt in him that he would go into the town; it was only a matter of the means that kept him pondering.

There might easily be a dozen men in Fairbanks who had journeyed up Candy Creek, who at one time or another had seen him and marked him, because of his famous inhospitality. Some might remember his dogs, since they were a memorable lot, indeed. Others would recall him, not so much on account of his size, for Alaska is the home of big men, but because of that close cowl of tawny beard that was fitted around his face. For nine long years his face had been bearded. Well, to begin with, he could leave that token behind him.

He had some soft soap, as always. Then he spent a long time whetting his knife to a razor edge, and with the soap and a pannikin of warm water he took off that beard without the aid of a mirror. He even managed it without once gashing the skin, getting off the hair with meticulously careful strokes, until at last his face was naked and cold in the wind. He was grateful for the hood of his parka, as he mushed on into the town, for he felt that there was something almost indecent about the bareness of his face. It would be somewhat difficult to confront other men while his face was lacking its beard.

The yelling of dogs showed him the way to a kennel on the very edge of Fairbanks, and there he left the team. He merely said, as the kennel man admired the trio, pausing to wonder over Masterman: "You don't have to yell at them. They're used to quiet talk. They've never been clubbed. And let me warn you that, if you have any trouble with this leader of mine, it'll be wise not to raise a hand on him. If you do, he'll cut your throat."

Then he went into the town. It was paved, lighted, modernized. At a step the wilderness was left far behind, and one entered the heart of civilization again. For nine years Oliver had not seen a pavement. He turned in at a clothing store and got rid of half of his little roll of gold in exchange for an outfit.

"The mirror's busted," said the clerk. "There was a fellow in here the other day who didn't like the way he looked in that mirror, and he kicked the whole face out of it."

"You tell me if the togs fit, then I don't much care," answered Oliver.

He got a soft felt hat, a brown suit that was only a little too tight across his shoulders, and a pair of soft-topped riding boots. They were the only footwear that seemed civilized to him.

The clerk, all this time, looked on him with a good deal of awe. "You been pretty sick, ain't you?" he asked, letting his eyes dwell on Oliver's face. "Fever, eh? That thins a man down . . . and whitens him a lot."

Oliver nodded, took the bundle of his discarded clothes—wrapped hard and small—and moved on. People who passed him in the street were apt to check their steps in order to look askance at him—and always at his face. He would learn the reason in the first saloon, and, since there were plenty of saloons in Fairbanks, he had not gone a block before he turned through a doorway and into a big room the whole length of which was repeated brilliantly in the mirror behind the bar. He ordered a drink, and then gripped the edge of the bar, suddenly, as he looked into a face that was not his own.

A mask of dark bronze was fitted across his forehead, nose, and eyes, running back a little distance to the point where it stopped sharply against the stone-white in which the rest of his face was worked. It was not strange that people on the street had paused to glance at him for an instant. No doubt they had seen such contrasts before, but hardly one so distinct and unmistakable as this.

Yet it was not merely the color that shocked Oliver. He remembered the smooth, handsome features, evenly browned by the keen sun of the southwest. In nine years he had not had a chance to look at that face clearly, and now he saw that the small knives and hammers of time had completely remodeled him. The curve was gone from his upper lip, continually pursed against the lower; his chin was thrust out; past his mouth ran a long line, deeply incised; the very form of his nose was altered to something more arched, more hawk-like; at the base of the jaw a small mound of muscle continually worked; and the eyes were settled well back behind the shadow of a frown.

The barkeep slid the gold piece away, pushed back a rattling quantity of silver in exchange. "You been out a few years, brother, eh?" he said, regarding Oliver's complexion.

"I've been out a while," admitted Oliver.

He swallowed half of his drink. Instantly, it cast into his brain smoky fumes, like those of a fire, and his lips worked because of the half-nauseating taste of the whiskey—a taste nine years forgotten. He asked for tobacco and wheat-straw papers. His fingers remembered well how to build the cigarette—how to tear off the film of tan paper, hold it as a trough in three fingers till the tobacco was sifted in, smooth that fragrant little heap of yellow flakes, turn the inner lip of the paper well under, catch it beneath the upper flap, twist the whole smooth and hard, moisten one edge so that it would hold fast, and turn over the end that was to take the fire. When he had made the smoke, he looked down at it a moment, wondering. His hands had done the whole thing, not his mind, yet for nine whole years he had not turned the trick.

He lighted it. A shower of sparks fell, and one burned unheeded into the weather-blackened skin of the hand that rested on the edge of the bar. A greater pain was preoccupying Riley Oliver's mind as he drew the first breath of the smoke deep down into his lungs. The old days were returning to him—the pale, brilliant skies of the Southwest, the dusty trails, the voices of the cattle reaching far out into the dim horizon, until the world and all life seemed to be filled with security and comfort.

The thin sweetness of the smoke mounted with the liquor to his brain and set vague sounds afloat in his memory. At first he knew merely that they were pleasant and melancholy with distance, then he recalled the bells of San Marco, ringing with deep vibrations over the river, or flinging high notes far across the hills. He had heard them many a time as he rode in from the ranch, the acrid taste of alkali in his throat, the lights of the town beginning to gleam and twinkle like stars through the valley shadows.

That was nine years ago, and now, at the end of the long trail, he stood in a barroom in the center of bleak Alaska, with danger to his life waiting somewhere behind his back. Again he looked into the mirror, and frowned more deeply at what he saw—for like a shadow beside that face masked in bronze he seemed to see the grinning, cheerful image of a man who was dead, a man across whose nose was a trail of freckles. For the first time it seemed to Oliver that he really had committed a crime when he pulled the trigger that ended that life of merry nonsense.

He decided that he was being a sentimental fool, for that good-natured deputy had been a traitor, after all—a traitor and a crook—and he had come to the proper trail's ending for traitors and crooks. . . . It was only that in life itself there is something sacred; Oliver could feel it in the wastage of his own nine years that could not be recalled, could never be recalled. They were gone farther away than the sound of the bells of San Marco, blown across the hills.

He lifted his head, suddenly, and looked about him, and it seemed to him that everywhere he saw happiness, security, and contentment. He had been only a kid, but he had taken nine years of hell, not prison. Nine long years, out of the pink of existence to which he never could return. Nine years? No, for every day had been multiplied by loneliness and hatred and despair. Remorse that had touched him today for the first time seemed to open the way to a quicker and a keener understanding of other men. All of these fellows who had such careless eyes were at ease with themselves and contented with others.

He himself had never been such a one. Even in those days when he had lived within sound of the bells of San Marco there had been a strain of grimness in him; he had looked, not at the face and substance of things, but through them—toward distant goals. That was why he had been able to take a human life and feel nothing but the clearing of an account, as he pressed the trigger of the rifle.

Melville, too, had something of the same strain in him. But Melville had submitted to the voice of the law when Willie Birch appeared. Riley Oliver was made of more flawless steel.

He caught the eye of a lad standing beside him, a youngster of nineteen or twenty, with a fine pair of shoulders, and as straight a pair of eyes as ever looked at danger with an untroubled mind. Riley Oliver had been about that age when he took the life of another man by the crooking of his trigger finger.

He smiled faintly at the thought, and the boy said instantly, taking up the token of friendship: "Have a drink, partner?"

Oliver looked at him again and felt infinitely old. "I can't drink another," he confessed. "I've been out for a long time, and the stuff socks me between the eyes."

The glance of the youth measured the poundage of his companion at the bar, and the weight of manhood behind that muscle and bone. He opened his eyes.

"I thought all of you old-timers could drink like fish," he said.

"We can . . . and then we're hooked, like fish, and fried . . . or boiled, maybe," said Oliver. He was uneasy as soon as he had spoken, for that word "hooked" suggested that the law might have a claim upon him—and there were officers of the law in Fairbanks. There was Willie Birch, for instance, and he was not the only one.

"Well, then," said the boy, "here's lookin' at you."

As Riley Oliver lifted his glass, the youngster was true to his word—his eye did not flinch from the face of his companion as the scalding stuff went down his throat.

"Jiminy!" said the boy. "Got a burn in it, ain't it?"

"A lot of fire and smoke, too," said Oliver. He felt strangely at sea in talking like this, lightly and carelessly. It was a novelty that made him want to spread his elbows at the board; in him, he suddenly realized, there were pent-up volumes of words and a deathless hunger for human language.

"I guess you're an old-timer, all right," the boy was remarking, his eyes still sparkling with eagerness.

"I've been around for a while," admitted Oliver again. "But not in Fairbanks, lately. Any news in town?"

"No, nothing much."

"Willie Birch caught the Jap yet?"

"Jap Laforge? Nobody will be catching Laforge, I guess. Not in any hurry, they won't! He cleaned up the Thompson brothers last month. The news just came in. Three dead men, back there, and four hundred pounds of gold dust that Laforge hauled away with him."

"Four hundred pounds! That's worth having!"

"Yeah, it sure is. Not even Willie Birch will be taking Laforge, I guess. Laforge is a devil. He gets away with things. Maybe anybody does, if he doesn't care how many he leaves dead on his trail. I guess blood greases the runners and makes everything pretty slick." The youngster shrugged his powerful shoulders, and then added: "But Birch just came in with a man."

"Oh, did he? What sort?"

"Bank robber. Fellow who's been away from the States for five years, hiding down on Candy Creek. Willie Birch brought him all the way here from Candy Creek . . . clean across the mountains. It must have been a devil of a trip, this time of year."

"Must have been," said Oliver. "Fight?"

"No. Birch got the drop on him. Birch had some other news, too. There is a sourdough down on Candy Creek who followed Birch's trail all the way to town, and almost caught him just outside of town. Nobody catches up with Birch on the trail, but this old-timer did it! Birch says he's as likely as not to come right into Fairbanks to try to help his friend Melville."

"How can they spot him?" asked Oliver carelessly.

"Why, he's a big fellow, dressed wild, and there's a description of his lead dog published all over town."

Chapter Eight

TAKING CHANCES

That announcement was enough to shake up Riley Oliver until the images of the lights trembled before him in the mirror like moonshine wavering across moving water. At last he said: "There are thousands of dogs in Fairbanks. Pretty hard to run down any special one, I should say."

"Not so hard," said the boy. "I'd tackle that job myself. All you have to do is just sit tight in a hotel, and ring up all the kennels and stables. Ask 'em if they've got on hand any dogs that weigh around a hundred and fifty or sixty and who look like purebred wolves. Maybe you might get one wrong lead . . . not more'n that. There ain't many dogs that would fit that heading."

"A whole lot of MacKenzie River Huskies run to that size."

"Yeah, but they don't look like timber wolves."

"It's true," nodded Oliver.

Far back on Candy Creek, when Birch had sent bullets at the great dog, the trail-man had got his first impression of the Masterman. He had a second impression by touch and by tooth, not long after. No wonder he was able to furnish a vivid impression of the loose leader.

"Kind of a wild man, I guess is what he is," the boy went on. "Think of him, comin' up the trail all that way on the run! Working his sled across the mountains . . . him with one pair of hands, and them with three. That's what Willie Birch says . . . this gent they call Doc is as strong as he's crazy. Kind of excitin', ain't it? I mean, him charging right on into Fairbanks, like that. Maybe he's somewhere in the town right now!"

"They know his name, do they?"

"He's a sourdough down on Candy Creek. One of them you read about, who wouldn't take in even a dyin' man . . . a real mean, low hound. They'd oughta dynamite the dug-out of every grouch like that. . . . Eh?"

"Maybe," agreed Oliver.

"A fighting fool, though," went on the boy. "Seems that he tackled the two of 'em . . . a big chap named Christy, and Willie Birch. He done for them both. Birch has just got his arm out of a sling, and Christy still has a bandage around his head."

"You saw them all?"

"Yeah, I saw them all at the jail when I took the girl over there."

"Girl?" echoed Riley Oliver.

"Why, Melville's girl, of course. She's been in town for a couple of months, waiting for a chance to start a search for her father . . . waiting for a clue to where she could find him. I met her in the Copenhagen Hotel, where she stays. And look at the mean luck she has. She wants to find her old man, and she finds him, all right . . . but in jail!"

Oliver went out into the street, where the long twilight was beginning. The thing began to seem like a set piece, now that the girl was on hand to see her father's ruin. He would have to find her, but something else needed his attention first.

He returned to the kennel, to find the burly proprietor outside of a small run that was fenced and covered with iron bars. He had a knotted club in one hand, and a bulldog revolver in the other. From his right shoulder to the wrist, his coat was ripped, and the sweater beneath it; blood stained the rags. Inside the run, in the exact center, lay the Masterman, his head raised, his eyes calm but green as the dangerous sea.

Passion gave swift recognition to the mind of the kennel man, and he knew Riley Oliver in spite of the changed clothes and the dim light. He broke into hearty curses.

"Gimme a dog . . . any kind of a dog . . . and I'll handle him like a lamb," declared the kennel man, shaking his club at Oliver's head. "Gimme a dog that's big, and the bigger he is and the meaner he is, the more he's my meat. But that thing in there ain't a dog. That's a cross between a three-headed snake and a gorilla, with a hot spot of tiger thrown in. Why didn't you tell me?"

"I told you not to lift a hand at him, and to keep your voice down. He wouldn't have bothered you, if you'd done those things."

"Oh, he wouldn't, eh?" said the kennel man. "You know so damn' well what he'll do and what he won't do, eh? I go in there to feed him, and, when I hoist a fish at him, damn me white, if he don't try for my throat. I done a quick dodge, but he got my coat and a slice of my shoulder, too. Lemme see *you* step in there and handle him."

A mere gesture brought Masterman gliding to the bars, and Oliver slipped his hand between them and dropped them on the great wolfish head. At that, the fury of the kennel man diminished suddenly; it took a new but milder turn.

"Whatcha mean by passin' me a trick dog?" he demanded. "You can take him . . . and the rest of 'em . . . and get out. Get out, or I'll throw 'em out . . . and you after 'em!"

But his words were stronger than his voice, and, looking into the square, brutal face, Oliver determined to take a chance, and a long chance. Perfect frankness and trust win more than dollars in the white north.

"Willie Birch will be on the telephone asking you if you have a hundred-and-fifty-pound dog that looks like a wolf," he remarked. "A dog that was driven in here by a tall man with sandy hair. I guess you've seen the dog and the man, too."

"Willie Birch wants . . . ?" began the other. He paused, squinting his eyes and parting his lips. "Who are you, brother, and what does Birch want you for?"

"I'm Riley Oliver. Birch wants me for killing a deputy marshal in the hills behind San Marco of the Bells, down there on the Mexican border, nine years ago. Ever since, I've had a cabin on Candy Creek."

The kennel men grunted as though a punch had jarred him. "You come in here with me," he muttered.

He brought Oliver into a scuffy little room where the air was damp with the stale sweetness of boiled tea and heavily fumed with pipe tobacco. From the ceiling hung an electric light, the globe almost frosted over with dirt. But on the table beneath it, as if to represent culture and good housekeeping, a red cloth was spread—a cloth with deep fringes, upon which were laid a pair of books, ready for the leisure of the gentleman of the house. A liver-colored Malamute with a soiled bandage about his head lay in the corner by the stove.

The kennel man put his gun on the table and spun his club lightly in the expert fingers of one hand. "Who sent you to me?" he asked.

"Nobody."

"Don't lie. Who sent you to me, Oliver?"

"Nobody sent me to you. I picked you for a white man, that's all."

"Yeah? The hell you did!" His frown puckered his fleshy forehead to the roots of his hair. "Go on and tell me, Oliver," he persisted. "Somebody tipped you off, and you come here.

It's all right, only I'd like to know who done the tipping."

"I'm telling you straight. I never saw you or heard of you before today."

"Your dog makes a play at me. I give you a damning. And that's what makes you think that I'm a white man, eh?"

"Well, you didn't shoot the dog . . . and you did your damning to my face."

The kennel man bit his lips, but grinned in spite of himself. "How come you plugged the deputy marshal down there at what-not?"

"He double-crossed me and got me jailed for his own dirty work. I got loose, and he took a posse after me . . . my horse petered out, and I shot him. That's all."

"You socked him, eh?"

"Yes."

The kennel man grinned again. "I guess we ain't gonna have no more trouble," he said. "There's things about you that I can understand, Oliver . . . and there's things about me that you can understand. If Willie Birch gives me a ring, I never seen a hundred-and-fifty pound dog in my life, and nobody your size has been inside my joint for a year. Is that right?"

"That's 'bout right. But there's one more thing . . . you won't get rich off me."

"Money and old fish . . . they both stink," said the kennel man delicately. "I'm gonna cover your trail, brother. You lay your money on that."

"One of these days," said Oliver warmly. But he checked himself and merely added: "Well, so long."

"So long," said the kennel man. He held out a hand that was covered with fish scales, grease, and dried blood, and Oliver gave it a mighty grasp and left the kennels with new hope. He understood that it was merely a rear-guard action that he had fought, but at least he had not been destroyed before the day of the great battle that was sure to come.

He found the Copenhagen Hotel. A phonograph howled in one corner of the lobby, and men sat about the center stove, reading old newspapers with hungry eyes, vainly striving to catch up with months or years of the outside.

The clerk observed him with a grin. "How does it feel to have your face back, partner?" he asked.

And as Oliver crossed the lobby to go upstairs to his room, heads were lifted, and voices murmured: "There's an old-timer." "Them feet can't forget snowshoes, yet." "Whiskey's gonna paint him red before morning."

None of those voices was raised, but he heard them with ears that had become sensitive by listening to the sounds of the wilderness, the secret and whispering noises.

He tipped the boy who showed him to his room, and, when the door had closed again, he looked around him at the walls and felt that they were moving in to hold him there, until perhaps Willie Birch and other men arrived, to rap heavily upon the door. With the vastness of the open country around Fairbanks all about him, it seemed utter madness to have walked into this narrow trap.

Melville's cause was not enough to bring him to this pass. Nothing was enough, for down yonder in San Marco of the Bells they had plenty of ropes with which to hang murderers.

The one drink of whiskey had been enough to parch his throat and set up a dull aching at the base of his skull. He turned on the cold water tap and let it run. It felt warm and would not run cold; the taste of the water was lukewarm, finally, and foul.

After all, that was civilization—a taint in humanity. Yonder, on Candy Creek, he had been surrounded by nothing except the work of his own hands, dogs of his own rearing, pelts of his own curing. A man could live and breathe in such a place as that. He could not help wondering how he had been dislodged from it, and, going back slowly over the events, he came to the moment when he stood at the door and heard the name of Steve Christy.

Well, it was one killing that had driven him into nine years of exile; a desire to give Melville his chance for a red accounting with Christy was what had brought on the whole confusion and disaster that followed. Perhaps some men could not exist in the society of others—he might be one of that number.

He began to scrub his hands, but it was hard and unsatisfactory work. Cleanliness had always been a major point in his life, but the fat and grease and oil that he had to work in as a trapper, the cleansing of guns and traps, had ingrained the black around his fingertips and in the creases of the calluses. The nails were broken short, or split, and they could only be roughed off, not trimmed to smoothness.

His nature, perhaps, was the same as those hands—fitted for life in the wilderness as a sort of superior animal, but not fitted for association with the polished men and women of the world. Among beasts he had importance; among men, he was a beast.

He crossed to the window, impatiently, jerked it open, and leaned out into the night. To that newly naked face of his, the wind was cold, but after the stale air of the hotel, it was incredibly sweet.

There were few people on the street outside. Most of the shops were closing, and, perhaps for that very reason, Oliver took peculiar note of a man who had been standing opposite the hotel, but who turned and went slowly away as soon as the window was opened. He followed that form, and saw it hesitate at the next corner, then look back. In a moment, the stranger was gone around the corner, leaving Oliver with an odd certainty that the final glance had been for his lighted window, and that the fellow was someone sent to spot him.

He closed the window and finished drying his hands thoughtfully. No one but Willie Birch would put watchers on his trail, and, if he were suspected today, he was fairly sure to be arrested tomorrow.

He threw the hand towel across the room, felt for the weight of the heavy Colt revolver beneath his coat, took up his hat, and went downstairs. **Restaurant** was painted over one door; the other led to the street, to the threshold of the great outdoors into which he could melt away and disappear, even from the hawk-like ken of a Willie Birch. But the savor of cooking was sweetly adrift in the air, and, suddenly, he turned toward it, resolved.

The shaving of his beard might not be a sufficient disguise. Even the new, closely fitted clothes might not be enough. But he was taking so many chances every minute now, that he would take a few more. If he were to liberate Melville, he had to remain in Fairbanks until he had formulated a plan. And while he lived in the town, it was necessary to eat.

Chapter Nine

NO BACK TRAIL

He found a small corner table and slid into a chair with a sigh. He had a feeling that not even his entry into Fairbanks had so deeply committed him to a dangerous course of action as his taking of that seat in the dining room, for from that moment every window, every door in the room was of vital interest to him—as a means of exit.

A waitress with a fat, pretty face and stained hands balanced herself on one foot in the midst of her rush to take his order. She started away as he mentioned soup and chops; he fairly had to shout to register the rest of the list, and she went off, nodding.

The warmth of the room began to make his face burn. He would have grown sleepy, except for that deathless hunger that was burning within him. He had lived well enough and through few periods of actual hunger during these years, but pea soup, chops, sausages, sauerkraut—during all that time he had not dined once on such noble dishes! His glance went down the menu, finding other items of delight, such as custard, chocolate cake, apple pie, gingersnaps! He had forgotten all about the bite and fragrance of ginger, but his mouth watered as the memory wakened.

He wanted to order everything on the card, but he knew that he must hold back, for a dog that eats too much for supper will not run well the next day, and he would have his running cut out for him before he was through with Fairbanks. He would have to handle his appetite like a typhoid convalescent.

That appetite consumed him more and more with every morsel he ate. It reminded him of a fable he had read somewhere, about the man in whom famine itself was lodged with a breath of fire that made whole banquets mere airy nothings.

A man stood up from the next table and shied his newspaper onto the floor.

Willie Birch Brings In Another, said the staring headline.

Oliver picked up the journal and read the full account. **Willow Birch had turned aside, for an instant, from the famous pursuit of the great Jap Laforge. Out on Candy Creek, far away, he had picked up a bank robber and defaulter wanted for five years in the States. Five years—but the net of Willie Birch collects criminals large and small. . . .** There was a great deal of this sort of thing, and then his own name, with a separate heading. **Southwestern Gunman in Fairbanks. Slayer of deputy marshal pursues Birch**, Oliver read.

It was all there—his name, Riley Oliver, his cabin on Candy Creek, his morose habits, the capture of Melville, Oliver's dangerous attack, his long pursuit of the two wounded men. The only rifle that Birch carried had been lost through the carelessness of his companion; he had been forced to flee at breakneck speed before Melville's friend, who was following. The muscles on Riley Oliver's jaws bulged when he read that. So he had been pursuing a man without a rifle, had he?

They had hoped to distance Oliver in crossing the mountains, but he had persisted with the strength of a giant. Twice, from great distances, the glass had picked him out. Only the thaw that widened the gulf between the two parties had permitted the trail-man to reach Fairbanks ahead of Oliver.

Once inside the city, with two dogs harnessed to a light sled, and with a hastily gathered posse, well-armed, Birch had rushed out to take up the back trail of the gunman. But behold, there *was* no back trail! Straight into the town the sign went on. With incredible boldness, this desperado had advanced until the paved streets completely destroyed all sign at once.

But, of course, a man and such a team could not disappear for long in Fairbanks. The team would have to be kenneled, as its leader was a giant among dogs, just as its driver was among men. Both would soon be at hand.

To this "desperado," as he read the account, there came two comforts. One was the resolute face of the kennel man who had pledged him his word and his hand. The other was that reference to his gigantic size, for people hunting a giant would hardly be likely to strike upon him, as he sat there at the end of his meal, drinking coffee and smoking his cigarette. It was not much of a shelter that secured him. It was very much like lying behind a mere riffle of snow when stalking game. Nevertheless, he deliberately relaxed until his head nodded. Sleep made a twilight in his mind. . . .

Suddenly he started. Something had touched his shoulder.

Out of his doze Oliver wakened to seize with a lightning movement—the soft wrist of the waitress. She was too frightened to cry out, and, before the noise could begin, she was between a gasp and a smile.

"I thought I was sleeping out," he explained hastily, "and a wolf got me by the shoulder."

She dropped the bill on the table. "If it had been a wolf, you'd've broke his neck for him," said the girl, rubbing the bruised place.

The tip she got was a cure-all.

Over a second cup of coffee and another cigarette, Oliver reconsidered the newspaper. Melville was in jail and had to be taken out—that was the short of it. He went into the lobby and warmed his back a moment before the big stove, for the night was turning cold and the wind that slithered through every crack touched one with fingers of ice.

"How long you been out?" asked a neighbor by the stove.

"I've been out so long," said Oliver, "that I'm ready for a winter's sleep."

This caused some chuckling and a good many comments. A man with a bald head and a fiery red beard started to tell a yarn about a Swede who had spent seven years at Point Barrow or on the ice, but his story and all other talk was brought to a pause when a girl crossed the lobby and went slowly, wearily up the stairs.

The sudden pause allowed Oliver to hear one man whisper: "Who's that?"

"The poor Melville girl," came the answer.

"I'm going to start that sleep right now," said Oliver, as the girl disappeared.

He strode across the room. A bawling noise followed him. "You can't talk to her. She kind of thinks that it's too far north to talk to a man."

But Oliver went on up the stairs with long strides, in time to see the swish of her furs as she went around a corner in the hallway.

He overtook her as she lifted a key into a locked door. At the sound or the shadow of his coming, she tried to turn the lock suddenly, failed, and whirled about with a frightened face to confront him.

"If you're from the newspaper," she said, "I can't talk for publication. I've told them that before."

The hood of the parka shadowed her face. He could only see that she was small and that she was frightened. Behind her, one hand still worked vaguely at the lock of her door.

He had stopped a stride away, and he answered now: "I'm not from a newspaper. You're Bob Melville's girl, I suppose?"

The lock gave, at last. She pushed the door open and shrank across the threshold.

"Yes, I'm Mary Melville," she answered with more confidence, now that she could throw a barrier between them at any moment.

"I'm a friend of Bob's," said Oliver.

She shook her head. "He has no friends . . . up here."

"He has one," insisted Oliver.

"Only . . . ," she began. Then she tilted back her head so suddenly that the hood of the parka slipped down onto her shoulders and showed to Riley Oliver a brightness of hair and face and eyes—a brightness that warmed his heart and started a thaw in that long, nine-year winter through which he had been living.

"There's only one . . . Riley Oliver," she murmured. She shook her head, and added: "He's a huge man with a tawny beard."

He passed a hand over the new smoothness of his skin, and smiled at her a little.

She came out a step to look at him more closely, but still she kept inside the threshold.

He went on to give his proofs. "We were introduced to each other, your father and I, with a pair of guns and a knife."

It was clear that Melville had told her the story, for she threw out both hands in a quick gesture. Suddenly she was smiling up at him. Her eyes widened. Her soul seemed to open and receive him. Up and down the corridor she cast a frightened glance, then drew him into her room. The upper air of that room was warmed by a stove that burned in one corner, a spot of dull red on one of its cheeks. But a layer of cold rose from the floor and chilled the legs as though one were wading in water.

She was closing and locking the door, and then she hurried back to him. She was half-delighted and half-frightened, but Riley Oliver was ill at ease. He had seen the opened bed, the blue flannel nightdress hung over the back of a chair to warm beside the stove. The frosted pane of the window gave to the room a guilty secrecy. So Oliver stood now by the small center table, resting the dark fingers of one hand on the edge of it and looking down at a half written letter that began: **Dear Mommy. . . .**

She was up here in the north, in the middle of the steel-hard business of life, but she was only a child. She ought never to have come here. Then he was embarrassed still more because he had stared at the letter, had caught a glimpse of the sacred privacy of her mind.

There was no embarrassment about her, however—only the excitement that made her burn. He wanted to look fullly at her, but he could not. He wanted to know whether her hair was golden or merely a pale, curling, luminous brown—and whether her eyes were blue or green-gray. But he could not look squarely at her any more than he had been able to meet the glance of the schoolteacher in those old days when every schoolroom riot was traced back to that young troublemaker, Riley Oliver.

"You *are* Riley Oliver," said the girl. "At first you looked too small, but you *are* Riley Oliver. And if you're he, how do you dare to be in Fairbanks . . . and, here, in this hotel? Don't you know that . . . ?" She paused, seeing that, of course, he must know how great his danger was.

"I hope to be leaving soon," said Oliver. "I've got a small job on my hands, and then I'm going to leave. I wanted to see you, first. I wanted to know what's inside the jail."

"I don't know," she said.

"But you've been there. You were there today."

"I didn't see anything but my father."

"How is he?"

"Gray . . . and older . . . and more glorious, more kind than ever. He told me about you . . . a lot. He told me how. . . ."

"Wait a minute," Oliver said, for he felt that his face was growing hot.

The air in that room suddenly stifled him, and he wanted to get as far as possible from this girl. She pretended to be excited about him, but somewhere in her heart she was laughing at him—his own heart told him so. He was playing the part of a fool, standing there by the table, and gaping down at his own fingers.

"Wait a minute," he repeated. "It's about the inside of the jail . . . it's about the lay of the land there that I want to know. What can you tell me?"

"So that you could go and throw yourself away, trying to set my father free?" asked the girl. Her voice choked away as she added: "He told me that you'd do that and give up your life, if you couldn't bring him away with you. Do you think he wants you to? He begged me to get word to you that he prefers to take his chances with the law. Oh, if he lost you, it would be worse for him than losing his life. He loves you, Riley Oliver. So do I, because I know that you'd die for him. That's why I want you to go away. . . . Go quickly. Go now and save yourself!"

She took his arm, and a tremor passed up it as she drew him toward the door. The tremor entered his body. Strength, and an impenetrable hardness of spirit that had been his during nine bitter years, now began to weaken. Something like self-pity stung his eyes. He felt a terrible shame and fear that she might see his weakness.

At the door, as she opened it, he tried to face her. All his eyes could make out, as he mumbled good bye, was something like a mist with a light in it. Then he stumbled down the hall to his own room.

No stove was burning there, but the damp cold of the air seemed to be choking him still, until he pulled up the window. The icy wind made it possible for him to breathe once more. It blew the vapors from his mind. When he closed the window again, he was aware in the silence of the room of the hurried and tremendous pounding of his heart, and a weakness in his knees. He felt a childish desire to go hurrying back to the girl and tell her what his symptoms were, and ask her opinion as to what had gone wrong. For she no longer seemed a mere child to him. Bob Melville's was the biggest nature and the staunchest soul that Riley Oliver had ever known among men, and yet, miraculously, Bob Melville was the father of such a woman as this!

He sat on the edge of his bed, gathering his strength, cursing softly and steadily, scowling into darkness, for he had not lighted the lamp. At length he was master of himself again, except for one bit of lonely and melancholy beauty in his soul.

Chapter Ten

MIDNIGHT CALLER

He pulled off his coat, stretched out on the bed, and set his mind like an alarm clock for three hours hence. At exactly that moment, therefore, he wakened, and found a tremor of cold in his body, his hands numb, the tip of his nose almost painful.

He did not light the lamp, for that window of his must remain dark. He merely swung his arms till the circulation started again, and, finding his parka in the gloom, he went to the window and worked it up silently.

A gush of wind entered and washed around the room, found a paper somewhere, and rattled it noisily. The hotel was full of similar sounds, for the breeze was half a gale, and with its gusts it was shaking the building to the heels. From the window he looked down the side of the wall and decided, for the second time, that a descent would be perfectly feasible. The street was empty in this block, although in the next one two men were entering a saloon, showing clearly for an instant under the brilliance of the electric light. Even a faint hum of music flew down the wind.

He closed the window again, with equal care lest it should grate, and in the darkness took off his coat, cut a great square of the black lining out of the back of it, and, still by sense of touch, threaded twine through two corners of the square. It fitted his head well, and he kept it on while he was cutting out the eye holes. Then he pulled off his shoes, donned the soft mukluks, and, with the parka twisted around his waist, he opened the window again, closed it behind him, and climbed down to the street, two stories below.

That was even more easily accomplished than he had expected. When he returned—if he did return from this night's adventure—the upward climb would be much harder. But now he knew every finger and foothold.

He donned the parka, put the mask in his pocket, and went straight to the jail. He had spotted it earlier that evening, a scant three blocks from the hotel. Now, in spite of the chill wind, he spent a whole hour investigating details.

The barred windows offered an incomplete ladder to the roof, but in the roof there was no skylight, probably, and even if there were, and he could gain the interior, he would not know where to find Melville. He tried to tell himself that there was time, since Melville knew that he was on the trail and would not throw his life lightly away. And tomorrow night would be warmer, perhaps.

However, a cool logic assured him that no time could be better than the present, for Willie Birch was not a fool, and neither Masterman nor his owner was an object easily hidden in a pocket. By tomorrow night the trail would have been run to its end, as far as he was concerned.

All of this was logical and simple, yet it was an hour before he stood, at last, at the door of the jail. He rang the bell. The mask was still in his pocket, but the hood of the parka was pulled well over his face when the three strong lights flashed on above and beside the door. One of these was no higher than his knee, and it seemed to be peering up into his eyes with a human recognition. He took a firmer grip on his revolver.

Through the very thick of the door a voice said: "Well, what do you want?"

"Lemme in," said Oliver.

"What for?"

"Got a message."

"For who?"

"Your boss," said Oliver.

"He's turned in."

"Wake him up, then."

"I'm likely to do that!"

"Going to keep me freezing here all night? I'll go back and say you would not let me in."

"Something important?"

"Important? You fool, what time of night is it?"

"Wait a minute. Who's it from?"

"Willie Birch."

A muttering of oaths followed, and then the bolts inside were drawn one by one. The door swung open a few inches, and, as the hand of the jailer gripped the edge of it, to keep the wind from forcing it suddenly wide, Oliver heard him say: "All right, where's the letter?"

"Here," answered Oliver. He had only a dim target—a shadow among shadows—inside the doorway, but he hit for what he thought to be the face, and stepped inside the panel of the door to catch the jailer as he fell. He held the slack of the body over one arm, pulled the door shut behind him, and laid the senseless weight on the floor. Then he slipped his mask over his face and tied the strings behind his head, unbuckled the gun belt of the jailer and put it a little to one side, and with a bit of twine that was always with him he tied the man's hands behind his back.

By this time, the other was half groaning, half gasping his way back to consciousness. Oliver lifted him to his feet and saw a pudgy face still groggy and loose-lipped from the effects of the blow.

"Wake up," said Oliver. "I want Melville, and you can show the way."

The other shook his head, staggered, and got his weight balanced on his legs at last. "You want Melville? Who's Melville?"

"Birch brought him in today."

"Oh, him." Understanding gradually brightened in the blue eyes of the jailer. "Look at . . . ," he said. "Whatcha wanna do?"

"Open the door of Melville's cell, and take him out."

"You can't wangle that. He's in the cellar."

"You've got enough keys in your pocket that will open the door," suggested Oliver. "I'm in a hurry." He kept his grip with one hand. With the other he laid the muzzle of his revolver on the chest of his captive.

The man twisted his mouth as he looked down at the gun. "I ain't got the cellar key," he said.

"Where is it?"

"The chief has it."

"Get it from him, then."

"Wait a minute here, and I'll get it."

Riley Oliver grinned. "You take me where your chief is," he said.

"It's gonna be hell," groaned the jailer. "All right. Come along down the hall."

He turned and went down the corridor, Oliver's hand still on his shoulder.

"Are you the gent who followed Birch in? Are you Riley Oliver?" whispered the jailer.

"Never mind. Where's your chief?"

"You're him, all right," sighed the other, ignoring the question. "You're Riley Oliver. And Birch told us to look sharp. He told us to have eyes in our heads. But how would I know that you would be fool enough to walk right up to the door of the jail, in the middle of the night? How would I know that, I ask you?"

"You wouldn't know," agreed Oliver.

The other paused in front of a door.

"This it?" asked Oliver.

"Yes."

"What's inside?"

"He's sleepin' on a couch, left of the door. There's a window straight on, an' a desk in the middle of the room. That's about all, except a coupla chairs."

"Door open?"

"Yes."

"I'll open it, but you go in first." He turned the knob of the door with delicate care, felt the latch disengage, and pushed the panel open upon profoundest blackness.

Chapter Eleven

THE STRENGTH IN WEAKNESS

No darkness is utter. Moving before the eyes there are always faintly outlined shadows that may be only of the mind. Like a hunter in a midnight forest, Oliver entered the room behind the jailer. He kept his hard grip on the shoulder of his companion as he shut the door behind him. Then he pulled his revolver and pointed it toward the left, where the couch was said to be.

There was a stove opposite the door, and, although the wood had burned low in it, out of a crack in the firebox a single ray of red light glanced on the varnished side of the desk and vaguely hinted at the outlines of objects in the night.

"Where's the light switch?" asked Oliver in a whisper.

"Right of the door," murmured the other with equal caution.

Oliver found it, turned it with the tips of his fingers that still held the revolver, and with the snap of the turning of the switch, brilliant light sprang into his eyes.

There on the left was the man he wanted, sitting bolt erect on the couch, a fur robe spilling away from him. The shock of fear had not struck him blank. Instead, it had contorted all the features of a bulldog face.

The jailer shrugged his shoulders, and jerked his head toward Oliver. "Gent come to make a call on you, Jennings," he said.

Jennings regarded the leveled gun, nodding.

"Stick up your hands, and then stand," commanded Oliver. "That's it. Go over there and pull down the shade of that window. Now turn your back to me, and keep the hands up. Stretch yourself, brother."

He disregarded the jailer for a moment, made him lower his hands behind his back, and secured them with another length of twine. He ran a few lengths about his body for extra security.

"That's all right, now," he pronounced. "Where's Melville?"

Jennings turned about. His face was crimson with a streak of white beside the mouth, like one whose heart is sick with weakness, or like one maddened with anger. In the case of Jennings, it was anger.

"Birch said you might come," he snarled. "And damn me if you ain't here! You let him in!" he added to the jailer, and his shoulders twitched as he tried to make a gesture to point his scorn. "You let him in, Bud, you cur!"

"Bud played out of luck. That's all," corrected Oliver.

"I played out of luck," muttered Bud. "He said he come from Birch. I didn't open the door no wider'n your hand, but he socked me. He's got an arm longer'n a leg."

"I want Melville," said Oliver.

"Go find him, then," suggested Jennings stubbornly, pushing out his jaw.

"You've got the keys, and you'll show me the way."

"Will I?"

"Yes."

"Try to make me, Oliver. You're Oliver, I guess."

"Where's Melville?" Oliver asked of Bud.

They looked like brothers, those two, but all the steel was in Jennings.

Bud winced. "Why . . . I dunno," he replied.

"Where's Melville?"

"Shut your mouth, Bud!" commanded Jennings. "I always

knew you were a yellow hound . . . a yellow hound is what you are! Shut your mug!"

"I dunno," gasped Bud.

"You'll know soon enough," answered Oliver.

He pulled open the door of the stove, and, as the warm breath puffed out at him, he picked up the poker and buried it in the glow of the coals. A tangled wreath of smoke issued and went trailing up toward the ceiling.

"My . . . my good God," breathed Bud.

"You sneakin' dog," said Jennings. "Shut your mouth!"

Oliver opened the draft and heard the air current begin to roar softly up the rusted chimney. He looked back over the room—at the guns racked against the wall, a small safe in the corner with gilded lettering across the top of it, a magnificent spread of moose horns on the wall above the desk. Jennings had pressed his lips together until the red stubble of beard was bristling.

"Don't be damning Bud," said Oliver. "*You'll* do the talking, partner."

"Will I? All right," said Jennings. "I'll do the talking, will I?" He threw back his head and laughed soundlessly. He shuddered. "That'll be pretty good . . . when *I* do the talking."

"You're the law, up here . . . you and the rest of 'em," said Oliver. "You hold the men here, and you're paid for it. I'd rather be a street cleaner, because here you treat *men* like dirt. You've kicked 'em around . . . you've slammed them with your fists . . . you've sneered at the poor devils who are scared and sick. That's the idea that fits you, Jennings. I know your kind."

"You know me, do you?"

"I know you, all right."

"You'll see how much you know of me. You think I'm a

yellow hound. But I ain't. You'll have a chance to see."

He swayed his head a little, side to side. He reminded Oliver of a bulldog, taking its hold and worrying that hold deeper. Bud had become a mere spectator, while these greater forces were at play.

"How many more of you in the jail tonight?" asked Oliver.

"None," said Jennings.

"You lie!"

"All right, I lie, then."

"How many more in the jail?"

"I told you."

"You'll talk pretty soon."

He glanced back into the stove and saw that the powerful draft had turned the red coals into a fiery gold that melted and gave out a shower of sparks, driving upward. When he pulled out the poker, the end of it was a bright orange with crystal sparkles adhering to it.

"You'll talk now," said Oliver. "Mind you, if you blat higher than a whisper, I'll kill you. I want Melville, and I'm going to have him."

He gripped Jennings suddenly by the lapels, and twisted them so that the strain forced back the man's head, freezing it in place. He thrust him against the wall and raised the branding iron.

"Are you talking, Jennings?"

Jennings's eyes, desperate with agony, fixed upon the trembling point of fire. "No," he gasped. "Damn you!"

"All right. You get it between the eyes, so the boys will know you."

A voice moaned from a corner of the room. That would be Bud.

But as the glowing iron came nearer, Jennings made a spitting sound like a cat. "Not on the face! I'll take it anywhere else! I'll talk! Get it away from my eyes!"

Oliver went back to the stove, put the poker beside it, closed the door, and like a good housekeeper turned off the draft again. When he turned about, he found that Jennings was leaning against the wall, looking into space.

"Now, where's Melville?" Oliver asked quietly.

In Jennings's stunned eyes appeared no understanding. But Bud gasped out hastily: "Cellar! He's in the cellar!"

"Melville's jammed into the cellar, eh?"

"That's where we keep the bad ones. Birch, he said you might come and make a try for him."

It was Bud who talked anxiously, his eyes upon the dumb, tortured face of Jennings. With sympathy and with a sort of incredulous horror he was staring at his superior.

"How many other men are in the jail?" said Oliver. "I mean, how many are blocking the way to Melville?"

Fear, it seemed, so choked Bud that he could speak no more; he could only shake his head for an instant. Still looking at Jennings, he said: "Nobody!"

"You sure?"

"Yeah . . . nobody . . . nobody."

"That's better. Where's the right set of keys?"

"Upper right hand drawer of the desk."

Oliver went to the desk.

Nearby, he heard Jennings whispering to himself softly: "I done it. I talked. I'm yellow."

The upper right hand drawer of the desk was locked, but the key was in the hole. Inside there was a piece of chamois, ragged with use, and black-marked here and there. Under that bit of cleaning leather lay a small steel ring with a half dozen keys strung on it. Oliver took them.

"I'm no good . . . I'm just a yellow hound," he heard Jennings whisper to his wretched soul.

"All right, boys," said Oliver. "We'll start. Do we have to go by way of the cell room?"

"No," said Bud, still fascinated as he watched Jennings. "We go down, right down into the cellar. There's a door at the end of the hall."

"Walk first, you two," said Oliver. "Keep shoulder to shoulder. Step soft. When you speak, whisper. Got irons on Melville?"

"Yeah," said Bud. "Wrist and ankle. That's the key . . . the smallest of 'em."

"And for the door?"

"The next one. It opens the two cellar doors, and the cell door, down there, too."

Closely herded before him, stepping before him lightly, the pair were taken into the hall by Oliver. They turned to the right, and at a door at the end of the corridor he found that the designated key fit.

They now stood at the head of a short, straight flight of steps, and, although the light was dim, he could see another door at the bottom, the metal of its lock glistening dimly.

Still he forced the pair before him like a living shield, and at the bottom of the stairs reached between them and unfastened the door. Of its own weight, or by the pressure of some imperceptible current of air, it began to open at once, untouched. Inside, a light turned, penciling long highlights on the bars of the cell, and throwing a regular pattern of shadows on the man who was stretched on the cot within.

He saw that. He felt Bud's body trembling violently. He recognized the bearded, upturned face of Melville, and then a cheerful voice exclaimed: "That you, Jennings?"

They had lied, then. A special guard, after all, watched over Melville. He saw Bud drop with a whimper to the floor, but Jennings hurled himself straight forward, knocking the door wide and diving on as though the cellar pavement were yielding water, to receive his body.

"Shoot, Barry!" screamed Jennings. "Shoot! Shoot!"

That outcry, piercing as a steam siren, ended at a stroke all chance of freeing Melville on this night, even if Oliver had not seen, at the same time, the form of the man named Barry before the door, a shotgun in his hands, the butt of it already settling into the hollow of his shoulder.

One frantic leap carried Oliver well up the steps as the first barrel of the riot gun boomed beneath him. He raced through the doorway above, slammed it behind him, and heard the entire jail awake with a roar that all of Fairbanks would listen to within a few seconds. When he pulled open the heavy burden of the front door, the steps and the street were empty. Into that emptiness he sprang, turned into the black mouth of an alley, and then checked his spring to a walk.

He had failed, but there was as much wonder as savage anger in his heart. He heard the town rousing, heard the slamming of doors, the running of feet along the pavements. Still, he concentrated on the mystery that had baffled him. How had Bud mustered the courage to lie, when Jennings himself had broken down under the pressure of the test? What strength of weakness had come to the jailer? So, in the midst of his tingling anger and that inward cold of disappointment, Riley Oliver was able to marvel, and to admire.

He reached the hotel to find many men in the street, but none of them watched the form that climbed up the darker side of the building, and then swung across from one window ledge to another until it disappeared.

Chapter Twelve

A TIPPED HAND?

He felt that the hotel was definitely a trap that would close over him, yet he remained there the next day, striving to make plans, and finding his brain empty as the hull of a wrecked ship. Although he sat for hours with a picture of the jail scrawled on a sheet of paper, and with the floor plan and the outside elevation carefully worked, so that every window and every door was located, no inspiration came to him. His usual inventiveness failed to respond.

There was a vast uproar over the affair at the jail, and the town newspaper printed the picture of the jail itself, of the special cellar cell in which Melville was confined, of Melville, the prisoner, of Bud, the jailer, and of Jennings, the expert gunfighter. That was not all, for the story of the raid upon the jail was illustrated by a bold genius in pen-and-ink who showed the predatory monster, Riley Oliver, stalking through the night, dashing open the heavily bolted front door, capturing the two guards, and penetrating to the bottom of the building, where that daring fellow Barry, standing unexpectedly in the way, had ruined the desperado's game with a riot gun.

The newspaper spilled that story all over three pages, with the illustrations to give it point. There followed it more stories that concerned the fruitless progress of the police search for the ruffian. Oliver did not need to read the newspapers to learn these things. The talk was always in the air in the hotel, in the streets, in the saloons, where bets were filed on Riley

Oliver, and against the state. Even with armed guards and strong walls, and with one success behind them, the guardians of the law were held at no better than one to three. Men said that Riley Oliver was biding his time, that he was working his way slowly, but surely. Such a man as he would burrow his way through frozen ground and come up through the jail like water through a well, people declared. There was absolutely nothing that would keep a man like Riley Oliver from dying for his partner, and he would do his dying inside that jail—men could lay their money on that. He would split the old building open and come out with his friend, or else he would die there, under the guns of the law.

Now, as he held this advertised devotion of his in contemplation, Oliver sometimes wondered at it himself. For what had Melville done for him, other than take a shot at him in the first place, and afterward sit by the fire, drink his tea, and eat his meat? Sometimes it seemed to Oliver that it was merely the imp of the perverse that worked in him, forcing him to remain in peril of his life in the town. But his purpose was unalterable.

In the evening he went to see his dogs in the kennel kept by Peter Harlaw, who was variously known by that name and as Pete the Dane, or Harlaw the Dane. That hardy fellow gave him a growl and a grin, and accepted a payment of gold.

"You been and raised hell, didn't you?" said Harlaw.

"I missed . . . that time," said Oliver. "How's Masterman?"

"Is that the four-legged chunk of misery that you call your leader?"

"Yes."

"He won't eat."

"I'll feed him," said Oliver.

Masterman came red-eyed to the door of the cage and

growled horribly at the sight of his master.

"He's off his feed. He's got the rabies, maybe. Stay out of there, Oliver," warned the kennel man.

But Oliver was already inside the enclosure, and Masterman had seized his hand in those great fangs, closing his eyes. He was moaning.

"Put up your gun," Oliver warned the kennel man. "He's only shaking hands."

So Harlaw went off, cursing quietly and wagging his head, to return with a great pan of fish. Oliver took it, but minutes went by before Masterman could taste it. As he watched, Oliver found a lump swelling in his throat—receding—and swelling again. For we cannot judge, in such matters as love, until after separations have been ended, and this was the first time he had been parted from the Masterman.

When he stood outside the cage again, he said: "I've been up inside the Circle . . . I just mushed in here the other day."

"Why should I know that?" asked Harlaw.

"They might ask me how I got to town . . . then they'd want to see the dogs."

"Suppose they saw *that* dog," suggested Harlaw, pointing.

"Drop a tarpaulin over the cage . . . they won't see him."

"Yeah, maybe I can do better than that," answered the Dane. He added: "I guess they'd trim me, eh, if they found out I was helping you, Oliver?"

"They'd trim you, all right," said Oliver.

"Would they?" repeated Harlaw, narrowing his eyes.

"They'd skin you alive," Oliver assured him.

"Well," growled Harlaw, "I'm just a fool."

"Sure you are," agreed Oliver. "Just a damn' silly fool."

And he went back down town with the feeling that his back was guarded.

★★★★★

In the hotel, in the saloons, he saved trouble by assuming a rôle of silence that was both natural and easily maintained, and it had the double value of enabling him to hear much at the same time that he avoided questions. A few days later, however, that faculty of listening got him into trouble.

He had noticed a big man with the brow of a bull and the eye of a pig who lived at his hotel, and who was usually easy to find because of the roar in his voice. His name was Baldy Wendell, although the thatch on his head was harmoniously dense all over. This fellow Wendell took it into his head that he would get information from Oliver that night after dinner, when the lobby was well-filled, when newspapers were rattling, and every man's pipe was going full blast.

He came through the rolling clouds of smoke that broke on his shoulders and swirled behind him and took up a position squarely in front of Oliver. He had his feet well-planted and his fists on his hips and his red face looked half merry, half brutally determined. Big as Oliver was, by two or three inches this monster out-topped him, and he had the mastery of eye.

"What's *your* name, boy?" he bellowed.

Oliver smiled and nodded, with much good nature.

"Go on," commanded the giant. "I'm Baldy Wendell. What's your moniker?"

Oliver smiled again.

"Better leave that dog alone, Baldy," called someone.

That gathered every eye to attention instantly, and Oliver felt the danger to be much like that when wolves softly steal up about an animal and sit down to wait for a kill. As Riley Oliver scanned the crowd quickly, he saw at the foot of the stairs a smaller form than the others. It was the girl, about to go up to her room, but frozen in place by the excitement that was filling the lobby crowd.

The sight of her cooled Riley Oliver. It enabled him to put far away the impulse to smash Baldy Wendell to small bits, for she was not the girl to be able to endure the sight of the beast that was in him. All the brightness in her eyes, as she looked across the shadows of the room toward him, was affectionate concern and admiration. He would not allow his own conduct to change that attitude.

Baldy had swayed his head about to glare toward the giver of advice. He exclaimed: "You mean this here is one of them strong and silent gents . . . is that what you mean? Well, that's all right, too, but I guess he'll talk, tonight. I like to hear gents talk out a little. That's the reason he's gonna tell us about himself. What's your name, eh?"

"It's on the register, yonder. It's Sam Deacon," said Oliver.

"You lie!" said the big man, who was apparently three sheets to the wind. "You ain't a deacon! You couldn't pass the plate!" He laughed loudly at his joke. "Go on, Sammy Deacon," he urged. "Lemme hear something out of you."

"Leave me alone, Wendell, will you?"

"No, I won't leave you alone! I'm tired of newspapers, and I guess you got news. Where'd you grow the beard that left you so damn bleached?"

"Up yonder," said Oliver.

"Where's up yonder?"

"Inside the Circle."

"What Circle?"

"The Arctic Circle, Baldy," someone put in.

"That's what you mean, Sammy, is it? Well, I been inside that Circle, too. And it ain't a dress circle, is it?"

Oliver shrugged his shoulders and turned away. He was caught and jerked back. His heel caught against an outstretched pair of mukluks, and he stumbled heavily against the wall.

Out of the distance, the voice of the girl cried out, thin and high-pitched like a bird's call. Two or three men of unsteady nerves jumped up from their chairs, for this was more than enough to cause a fight, but Baldy Wendell roared loudly: "You gotta handle your feet better'n that, to be a Circle man!"

If a bullet struck him between the eyes, thought Oliver, it would leave the gaping grin of the mouth to turn sodden and loose. Or if a well-placed fist, with certain poundage in motion behind it, landed in the middle of that smile, the thick lips might be split against the teeth.

He closed his eyes, steeled himself to endure, and drew in a breath. Above all things, it would be fatal if he allowed this madness to close in a red wave over his brain, for he must remain an unknown in Fairbanks.

As he looked out again, the giant roared with mirth again, saying: "Look how white he is! Don't be scared, Sammy. I ain't gonna hurt you. I just wanna know where you been inside the Circle. Far as Nome?"

Oliver moistened his lips. It was becoming hard to breathe.

"Come on! Answer up!" thundered Baldy Wendell. "Talk up!" he exclaimed. "You tryin' to make a fool out of me?"

It was not a red wave, but a light that snapped on in Oliver's brain. Suddenly he was aware of every muscle in his body, of the tremors in his arms, the tense knots that were forming over his abdomen.

"People can see for themselves," he said huskily.

"What?"

"People can see for themselves."

"See what?"

"That you're a fool."

"That I'm a . . . ? Oh, is that it?"

The teeth of Wendell set in a yellow line across the middle of his grin, as he stepped in with a ponderous fist. Oliver slid under it and clamped his arms around the big, solid barrel of a chest. It was a huge weight, and an active one, but he had lifted clumsier burdens than this that he heaved shoulder-high and hurled among the chairs with the swing of his body.

That bulk rose again with a face dreadful with amazement and rage. He was a trifle stunned, though, by the fall. And through the uproar that closed around his ears like substantial waves, Oliver ran lightly in and split the lips of Baldy on the hard anvil of his fist. Baldy Wendell sank slowly to his knees, reaching out with his hands to find the light that was gone from his uncomprehending eyes. His head was jerked backward by the hair, and above him appeared the white face and the bronze mask of Oliver. That sobered Wendell more than a plunge into an icy river.

"D'you know enough about my travels now, Baldy?" asked the husky, purring voice of Oliver.

"Yeah," breathed Wendell softly. "I know . . . enough. Lemme . . . lemme go."

"Why, of course," said Oliver.

He went back to the place where he had been standing before, and watched the big fellow go floundering through a mist, strike heavily against a side of the door with his shoulder, and so pass from the room.

Beyond that beaten fellow, Riley Oliver was very dimly aware of a small form that went up the stairs, slowly. A girl who helped herself by pulling at the banister with one hand. Her face was turned toward him, but he made out no features, only a certain whiteness. For half of his human intelligence was gone from Oliver, and in its place were his more brutal instincts, brutally working. It was as though he had eaten, but not his fill.

The hotel clerk was in the midst of the chaos, by this time, spouting questions, picking up chairs. He was surrounded by a grave silence in which, as Oliver noted, men carefully avoided his eyes.

For his own part, Oliver made it a point to roll another cigarette and smoke it slowly, always looking down at the floor, for he had a fear lest the others might glance in upon the savage tumult that was still in possession of his soul. Little by little he mastered it, and, reviewing all that happened, he could assure himself that he had not given away his hand. A huge, clumsy rough had charged him; he had upset the man with the commonest of wrestling devices. He had then stopped a wide-open rush with a straight right. That was all.

Yet, if that were all, it was strange that the other men in the room were still so hushed—strange that their mouths were now set rather crookedly, and that faint shadows of apprehension were on every face. One might have thought that they were looking at a dead man on the floor, covered by the guns that had performed the murder. They should have laughed—a few of them—and one or two of them would surely have been tempted, in the ordinary course of things, to remark that Baldy had something like this coming to him, that his fall was overdue.

What had happened, however, apparently, had not been the ordinary course of circumstances. For Riley, at least, it had been rather horrible. He would have been glad of so much as s single word, but it failed to come. Presently, finishing his cigarette, he went up the stairs.

Chapter Thirteen

THE FERRET'S FACE

There was still an animal tenseness in Riley Oliver as he went up the stairs after this scene. Only one regret, really, was in his mind—the dread lest he should have called too much attention on himself by the manner in which he had handled Baldy—but he was not inclined to take the thing too seriously. What town in Alaska had not seen hundreds of far worse brawls than this?

Yet, a fire and a song were in his brain as he went up the stairs, and in the darkness at the head of them he thought he saw a form that leaned over the inner banister. That shadow, if it were one, seemed to shift or fade like a dim thought from before his eyes.

Riley Oliver sprang to the hall level, and in the dull light of the single oil lamp that burned far down the corridor he actually saw a small figure fleeing. It might have been a poor mouse, scurrying before a cat. So, with a bound, he overtook it. If this were the spy of Willie Birch, or of the marshal's office of Fairbanks, something would happen to the fellow on the spot.

He had stretched out his hand when the running form flattened itself against the wall and turned on him a white face of fear. The girl!

He remembered now, how he had seen her watching. Then, in the blood-red excess of his passion, when Baldy Wendell had been beaten, the white face had gone up the stairs through the shadows. It had been she all the while. Now he stood over her like the brute that he was, with his hand actually grasping toward her throat. The burning of the lamp gave light enough only to guess by, rather than to see. Therefore, he trusted that she might not have seen the devil in his face.

He stammered something over her, but all that she answered was a rhythmically moaning sound.

He took her by the arm. Her whole body followed weakly, like the jointless body of a weak child, as he drew her a little toward the light. Her head fell back. That was like a child, too, to weep shamelessly—with no attempt to cover her face.

He looked through a thousand years of wonder at the trembling of her lips, and at the way the tears ran swiftly out from under the lashes. An artist would have painted a face like that to represent grief, because sorrow had not deformed it.

"Stop it! Stop crying, will you?" he demanded.

"I couldn't help it. I was afraid. I thought you were going to kill him. Afterward, I was afraid that they'd all kill you, if they could. I was watching, to see."

"Why should they have killed me, Mary?"

"I don't know."

"You do know." He shook her a little by the arm, and her head wavered from side to side.

"I don't know," she insisted. "I was afraid."

"You were afraid they'd kill me? Tell me why."

"Because of the way you fought. Because the way you fought would surely tell them that you're Riley Oliver!"

"Hush!"

That stopped her weeping suddenly.

"Ah . . . did anyone hear me?" she gasped. She laid a hand flat against his breast, and looked anxiously up and down, into the dim places of the corridor.

"Nobody heard you," he answered. "Stop trembling, Mary. *You* are not afraid of me, are you?"

"Oh, no," she said.

It seemed to him that he had to know the truth about that. It seemed to him that there was nothing in the world so vastly important as to learn whether or not she actually had been afraid of him. So he crouched until his face was level with hers, and he laid his hands about her head to steady it, so that she would have to look straight back at him.

Her head was absurdly small, and his thumbs came out under her chin. Through the softness of the flesh, he could feel the chin bone, a fragile thing that he might have crushed with a single grip.

"When you stood there watching, you weren't afraid of me?"

"No," said the girl.

"When I was fighting with Wendell . . . when I knocked him down, I mean, and sort of went after him . . . you weren't horrified and disgusted then?"

She closed her eyes. She shook her head as hard as she could from side to side, and the delicate touch of her cheeks caressed those iron-hard palms of his. She smiled at him to give the greater assurance, although he saw a crookedness of effort in that smiling.

"How could I be horrified or disgusted by you, Riley?" she asked. "I'm my father's daughter, am I not? How could I do anything but love your great soul?"

"Yet you're still trembling."

"I was afraid that they'd come rushing at you all at once, and all together. The way you made a child of that terrible, huge man, I thought they'd surely know you were the man who'd driven Willie Birch and Christy from Candy Creek and across the mountains. It seemed to me that they would *have* to know. . . . I'm not trembling any more, now. I'm as still as a stone."

As she spoke, she was in fact as quiet as a stone, and she smiled at him. The light seemed to grow dimmer. He felt a darkness of passion that drew him toward her. To resist this, he took his hands from her face and straightened to his full height. Her head tilted back a little, so that she could still watch him.

"It's true," said Oliver. "I'm going to believe that you weren't afraid, and that you didn't think me a beast . . . running amok."

It seemed that she had to close her eyes every time she shook her head in denial. By the delicate flicker of a shadow at the side of her throat, he made out the speed of her racing pulse.

"If they were to see us standing here, then they might guess that Bob Melville means something to both of us. Go to your room, Mary."

She nodded and turned down the hall, and he went with her, mightily drawn. He walked close to her. If her heart was beating as that pulse at her throat had been beating, he wanted to put his hand about her and feel the rapid pulsation. That would have a meaning to him. Everything about her had a meaning. Wherever the foggy dimness of light let his eyes touch her, he found meaning more than a thousand words. Her hair gleamed like a most ghostly halo.

He wanted to put her in a chair in the sun, in a house among the hills of San Marco. He wanted to keep her there quietly while they listened to the bells of San Marco. She became a part of his longing for his homeland. That pain of desire for his country had made a spacious place in his heart, and into that place she entered. Hereafter, to the end of his life, whenever he thought of the hills of San Marco—when he saw the white town beside the river, when he smelled the tarweed, or saw the doves rain down from the sky toward a creek at the close of the day, he would see this girl. She would watch it all, standing beside him. She, in her silence, meant as much to him as the music of the old bells of the mission church.

At her door, when she stopped, she turned to him and said: "When I knew what you had tried to do at the jail, I was certain that even you could never dare to stay here in Fairbanks. But my father knew better. He said that you would never give up unless I found you and begged you to go away . . . in his name. He told me to swear to you that he begs you to go away. He loves you, Riley! He told me that you're more than his flesh to him . . . and more than his own son. When I go to him tomorrow, may I tell him that I have your promise to go away?"

"I'm going to go soon," said Riley Oliver. "You can tell him that I won't be long in the town. Good night."

He found her hand and raised it to his lips, pressed it hard against them, twice. Then he felt the hand draw away, and she, too, was drawn away. The door closed and left a blankness before his eyes.

He went to his own room. There was still a faint ache in his throat, and it had been there ever since the moment when he had kissed her hand. He could remember. There had been a sound in his ears, at that moment, and it must have come from his own throat.

That, no doubt, was what had made her slip suddenly away from him. Perhaps the memory of it was making her tremble now, as she stood there between the frosted window and the door.

He lighted the lamp. Blood, he saw, had spurted across the knuckles of his right hand. Some of his own blood was welling from a slight cut. There was even a trace of it inside his fingers. If the girl were now looking down at the hand he had kissed, she would find it stained with red.

He washed the blood away with cold water. He sat down on the chair to pull the boots from his icy feet, and it was then that he heard a faint sound in the hall. It brought him to his feet with a start. He recognized the sound of a stealthy footfall on the flooring boards. Had the girl come back to add one word?

Then the door was thrown open, and he saw on the threshold a small man with a face that drew to a point in the long nose—a man with the face of a ferret—the face, in short, of Willie Birch!

They had come for him, then? Behind Birch loomed a larger pair of shoulders. In the darkness of the hallway was the face of Steve Christy.

Yes, they had come for him, and, if he pulled a gun on them, the girl would have the pleasure of seeing his dead body laid out on the floor.

"Hello, partner," said Birch. "Can we come in?"

"You seem to be coming. What's the idea?" asked Oliver.

"You're Sam Deacon, ain't you?"

"Yes, that's my name."

Was it possible that the lack of his beard and his different clothes made them uncertain of his identity?

"He says he's Sam Deacon," nodded Birch, "and, if that's a fact, then I guess we've opened the wrong door."

He seemed to be addressing his companion as he said this, but now he drew a revolver and added: "The fellow we're looking for is Riley Oliver. I think you're the gent we want."

Chapter Fourteen

DOWN FROM NOME

Willie Birch was capable of but two facial expressions, one of which was keen determination and the other a rather mocking smile. In either case, the stretching of the lips was the same, and so were the wrinkles in his thin cheeks. The difference lay only in the puckering about the eyes. But in Riley Oliver there was no doubt whatever—he would not even have needed the glimpse of the revolver to tell him that trail-man Birch felt he had set his teeth in a morsel worth having.

Oliver replied to the questioner. "All right, Birch. You'll want me in jail, then?"

"Own up to the name, do you?" asked Birch.

"No."

"Gonna make as much trouble as you can?"

"Why, I don't know," replied Oliver. "I've been out a long time, and I haven't made a stake . . . yet. I'd as soon rest in the jail as any other place."

Birch went to the window and sat on the ledge of the sill. "Got some guns?"

"Yes."

"Trot 'em out."

Oliver had a shining Colt on the table.

"Hand-polished," commented Christy.

"Know that Colt?" asked Birch of Christy.

The latter looked at Riley Oliver rather than at the gun, as he crossed the room to the weapon.

"I know that pair of eyes," he said. "I know the shape of

that head, too. That's Riley Oliver."

As he picked up the Colt, still staring at Oliver, he sneered savagely. "You had your little hand to play, and you played it for all it was worth. You chased us over the hills, eh? But we'll do the chasing now, Riley. Damn your heart, I could eat it raw! I could eat it without salt and pepper!"

Riley Oliver endured the tirade without impatience, for something told him that Willie Birch, at least, was not altogether clear as to the identity of his prisoner.

"You're under arrest," said Willie Birch. "I'm from the marshal's office, here in Fairbanks. Anything you say can be used against you. You know that?"

"I've heard that."

"Where have you heard it?"

"You mean, where have I ever been arrested?"

"Yes."

"I never was arrested."

"That's good, too," grinned Christy. "Never was arrested . . . never saw the jail in San Marco, eh?"

Oliver nodded at Christy. "The big boy doesn't seem to like me," he said. He kept his voice loud, almost bawling. That was the only effort he made to disguise it. The voice that both of these men had heard him use before had been a quiet voice, except for a few barking commands. So he kept forcing his voice for loudness. It thrust the sound more into his nose. It made his whole manner more aggressive, putting a swagger into his shoulders as he talked, moving his head a bit from side to side, in an assured way.

Perhaps Willie Birch had made up his mind, but at any rate his eyes were still studious.

"I don't like you," Christy had roared in answer. "What's more, I'm going to see the end of you! I'm going to see you hanged! You hear me, Oliver?"

Riley Oliver sprang to his feet, apparently disregarding the gun with which Birch followed his movement. "You big bleary-eyed son-of-a-bitch!" shouted Oliver. "Call me Oliver again and I'll take that gun away from you and shove it down your dirty throat . . . butt first!"

At this outburst, Christy had backed up a little, pointing the revolver toward the prisoner. He steadied himself, peering curiously at the purposely convulsed face of Riley Oliver.

"Shut your mouth," he said. "Or I'll knock the teeth out of it."

"That's enough, Christy," broke in Willie Birch. "You know that gun?"

"Sure I know it," said Christy sullenly.

"Wait a minute. Do something for me?" asked Oliver of the little trail-man.

"I don't mind, maybe," said Birch. In his attitude there was no rancor; there was a bird-like brightness and detachment about him.

"Tell him to put that Colt on the table."

"Put it on the table, Christy, will you?"

"Why should I?"

"Just because I asked you to."

Christy laid down the weapon. He scowled at Riley Oliver, as though this small victory enraged him.

"Now make him turn straight to you," suggested Oliver.

Christy did so, without waiting for the command from Birch.

"He's trying some low dodge on us," said Christy. "Watch him, Willie."

"Oh, yeah. I'll watch him like a father," said Willie Birch. "What's on your mind, Oliver?"

Riley Oliver thrust out an arm, thrust out a quivering forefinger. "*You* calling me that name, too? My name is Sam Deacon, and be damned to you!"

"All right, all right," said Willie Birch. He frowned as he spoke, seeming to find the affair very distasteful. "What's in your mind, anyway?"

"That big, wall-eyed buzzard," said Oliver loudly, "says that he knows that gun of mine. He's a liar. He never saw it before. Let him up and tell you *how* he knows it? What's the mark or the sign on it?"

"Go on," urged Birch to Christy. "Go on and tell us, Steve."

"Going to cross-examine *me*, eh?" snarled Christy, dropping his head a little, after a way that he had.

Riley Oliver's lean, savage face smiled. "Make him talk," he said.

"It's one of the guns that I saw in his cabin, down on Candy Creek . . . You know it's one of the guns you had on Candy Creek!" he added, whirling on Riley Oliver.

Oliver answered: "I never heard of Candy Creek. It's a fool name . . . and a fool that's naming it, as far as I can make out. But I'll show you something real about that gun!" He made a hasty stride across the room.

"Don't touch that Colt," said the quiet, rapid voice of Birch.

"I don't need to touch it. I know you've got the drop, Skinny. But I'll point out something. You see the heel of the gun? It got that dent by being banged on the head of a low-down guy in San Antone, and it's going to get another dent when I whack you over your skull, big boy! If you ever saw that gun, you saw the dent in the heel of it. Talk up! Tell Skinny that you're a liar, will you?"

Christy rubbed his knuckles up and down on his trouser leg. "I'm going to smash his face in for him," he said, half to himself and half to Birch.

"Leave him alone," answered Birch. "You can't identify the gun, then?"

"Maybe not for a judge and a jury, but I know that I've seen it before."

"Look here," cautioned Birch. "I'm leaning on you pretty hard for testimony, but you want to be careful what you say. Understand? Don't talk more than you know."

"You seem to have some sense," observed Oliver to Birch. "You might tell me what I'm pinched for, then."

"Murder," said Birch.

Oliver grunted with a violent start. "Murder," he repeated, under his breath. "Murder of whom?" he demanded loudly.

"A deputy federal marshal . . . a fellow called Sandy Wiegand. You're accused of shooting him."

"Never heard of him," said Oliver.

"Any half-wit can have sense enough to say 'no,' " observed Christy. His crimson face was still working, after his recent rebuff.

"You never heard of San Marco, either, eh?" asked Birch.

"No, never did. . . . Wait a minute. Hold on. There's a place called San Marco on the Río Grande," answered Oliver. "Want to hang me for knowing that?"

"That was a good try you made for Melville last night," broke in Christy.

"It was a good try, whoever made it," answered Oliver.

"Why are you tryin' to hold out?" asked Birch.

"Oh, I don't know. . . . This fellow Riley Oliver is due to hang if he's caught, isn't he? Maybe that's one reason I'll hold out, if I can."

"We've got the case on you pretty straight, Riley. I've looked over this town pretty careful. You're the only gent that looks about his size and age and weight, that come to Fairbanks on the right day, and that goes to bed early enough at night. A fellow has to have something on his mind when he turns in as early as you do, Riley." He snapped suddenly: "Keep your hands still!"

"I was after the makings."

"All right. But make it a slow reach."

A slow reach, accordingly, it was. Oliver built his cigarette with rapid fingers. He hoped they had eyes in their heads to mark the steadiness of his hands, not eyes that could look into the whirling confusion of his mind. He knew that he had only one hope. And that was to be hiding nothing, to affect an air of total unconcern, and to speak with a casual swing to his words.

"You boys want to know what parts me from Riley Oliver?" he proffered, as he lighted up and snapped out the match.

"You can loosen up and tell us," agreed Birch.

"Well, I'm only six feet, three, and about two hundred pounds. That's enough difference, isn't it?"

Birch shook his head. "What else parts you from him?"

"He lives on Candy Creek. I've never been there."

"No?"

"No."

"You're from where?"

"North, brother."

"Far as Nome?"

"Yes.

"You dig in Nome?"

"No. Nome dug in me. It took two years of digging out of me in a week."

Birch grinned. "How'd you get down here, then?"

"Dogs."

"That's a long trip."

"I'm used to long trips."

"Where'd you put up the dogs?"

"Fellow named Harlaw."

"Pete the Dane?"

"Yes."

"We'll go there and have a look-see," said Birch. "Got the big leader there, too?"

"My leader's not so very big."

"No?"

"No."

"Well, we'll have a look. I don't want to walk you through the streets in handcuffs."

"Thanks."

"I'll just borrow your gun. Fan him, Christy, and see if he's got any more artillery on him."

The fanning revealed no other gun, so Birch and big Riley Oliver walked out into the hall, with Christy behind them.

The hall was more brightly lighted than it had been before, because two or three lanterns were out there, borne by curious men who were eager to learn what had happened in Riley Oliver's room. They mattered very little to Oliver. What shocked him was the sight of Bob Melville's daughter. Willie Birch spotted her at once, and Oliver's heart sank as the man of law hailed her.

Chapter Fifteen

IS HE—OR ISN'T HE?

"You're Miss Melville? Bob Melville's daughter?" asked Birch eagerly.

"Yes," said the girl. She seemed about to shrink away through the crowd, but Birch's pointing forefinger fastened her to the spot.

"If you're Bob Melville's daughter," went on Birch, "then you know his friend, here . . . Riley Oliver?"

Oliver looked right and left, but saw no escape, unless with a sudden lurch he might be able to make the head of the steps and plunge down them, involving so many people in his fall that Birch and the rest would not dare to fire on the rolling mass. That chance, decided Oliver, was about one in a hundred.

Then he heard the girl saying: "I've heard my father speak about Riley Oliver, but I've never seen him."

"You mean to say?" exclaimed Birch, "that this . . . this man here . . . is not Riley Oliver?"

Oliver heard her answer. "I've seen that man in this hotel. I've seen him . . . brawling . . . in the lobby just this evening. That's all I know about him. I think his name is Deacon."

She spoke with care, as though she did not wish to make her disgust too apparent. Her lip curled. There was a lifting of one shoulder as she made a gesture that shut her away from all men of the "Deacon" ilk. It was almost too well done. It was enough to shake even the faith of Riley Oliver, to see the cleverness of this action—except that he knew it was done to save his life.

"That's a lot of folderol," burst out Christy in a loud voice. "A lot of bunk! She knows him. That's why she looks so white and scared!"

The girl looked straight into Christy's face. Then she said, to Birch, recognizing in him the authority to command: "Must I stay here any longer?"

Birch hesitated only a moment. Then he shrugged his shoulders. "You can go back to your room, Miss Melville. But if you don't mind, I might drop in and have a chat with you, a little while later."

As the girl nodded and turned away, Riley Oliver found himself marching down the stairs with Birch behind him and Christy before him. A loathing seized him as he looked at the head and shoulders of Steve Christy.

Other men were running up the stairs to get to the center of action. They turned and went slowly down again, staring over their shoulders at the prisoner.

"*That* ain't Riley Oliver," said one voice clearly. "I seen Doc Oliver down on Candy Creek. He's three inches taller and thirty pounds heavier than this here gent, and he's got a beard all over his face. Riley Oliver would eat this fellow Sam Deacon for breakfast . . . and not think that he'd fed any too well, either."

When they got out into the street, the crowd left them, merely rolling a few steps past the door of the hotel and then coming to a stand.

"We'll start shooting if you start moving fast, big boy," said Birch.

They turned a corner into a cold wind.

Oliver said: "What gave you the bright idea that I'm Riley Oliver?"

"Why, Oliver's a cross between a set of steel springs and a steam engine, what I hear about him, and you cleaned up Baldy Wendell like he was fried potatoes. Baldy is quite a lad, too. I've seen him tackle a whole roomful of gents, and wipe the platter clean. That made you look like Riley Oliver, to me," answered Birch.

"Thanks," said Oliver. "I don't mind getting famous in a Fairbanks way, as far as that goes. How do you feed in that jail?"

"On the fat."

"It suits me, then."

They went into the yard of Harlaw the Dane. Harlaw's voice, piping high with anger, was yelling and cursing in the distance. It approached and dissolved into a few growls as he saw his visitors.

"I wanna have a look at the leader of the dog team this gent drove in," said Birch. "That great big devil that looks like a wolf."

"His dogs are his dogs," said Harlaw. "How do I know which is the leader? I ain't a mind reader."

"No?" said Birch. "The last time I seen you, Pete, you could tell a leader from a sled dog, any time. You didn't have to see a team strung out. . . . But let's have a look at his outfit."

Carefully Oliver avoided the eyes of the kennel man, as the latter led them to a pen that held several Huskies. The dogs lay still, in a huddle, and with their red-stained wilderness eyes they stared back at the men who watched them.

"Where's your leader in that outfit?" asked Birch.

"Budge!" called Oliver. It was the sled dog he named. Once he had tested him as a leader.

A yellow-gray dog with sooty markings rose from the huddle and leaped to the fence.

"Yeah, he seems to know his name, anyway," agreed Birch. "But that don't make him a leader."

How could Birch know about the hundreds of miles during which the Masterman had ranged ahead, a loose leader, and Budge had swung the team?

"Make him do something," suggested Birch.

Oliver waved his hand. The big dog retreated with a bound to the farther side of the pen. He turned right and left in answer to mere gestures.

"Yeah, and that's all right, too," said Birch. "A fellow like you would have good dogs, or he wouldn't have none at all. But we'll look around. There ain't anything here that matches the hundred-and-fifty pound idea that I've heard about. Where is it, Harlaw?"

He turned grimly on the Dane, and the latter grunted: "I dunno what you're talkin' about."

"What's the name of this gent?" asked Birch.

"The moniker he gave me was Deacon."

"Show me the rest of the dogs."

They looked over the yard, rapidly. They came to the extra cage with the tarpaulin over it.

"Take that cover off, Harlaw," commanded Birch.

"There ain't anything there," said Harlaw.

"Take it off!" insisted Birch.

Oliver's eye turned slowly toward Birch. He knew where the trail-man wore his gun, and if he got that—well, the fight would be started. Harlaw stepped forward and snatched the tarpaulin from the cage. As Oliver flexed his body to spring, he saw, with bewilderment, that Masterman was not in the enclosure.

"Whatcha been doin', Harlaw?" snapped Birch. "Covering up a nice empty chunk of air with that tarpaulin?"

"I throwed it there, and there it lay," answered Harlaw.

"Any law ag'in' doin' that?"

"What's in the house?"

"Some grub, a table, a cloth on the table, a spread of horns, a coupla guns, some firewood. . . ."

"All right. No dogs?"

"Yeah."

"Yeah what?"

"Dogs."

"Harlaw, you don't win any votes from me, acting like this. What dogs are in there?"

"Dog with a sore head, and one that's comin' on with rabies, I think."

"We'll see 'em."

They walked into the house, and, as they went, Harlaw flicked his glance once at Oliver, a whip-stroke that left a mark on Doc's mind. That look meant, clear enough, that Masterman was housed in a room in the shack—he must be the dog "comin' on with rabies."

As they stepped into the main room, the Husky with the bandaged head stood up by the stove and growled at the stranger.

"That's not what I want to see," remarked Birch. "Where's this mad dog you talk about?"

There was a barely perceptible pause in the answer. It was just that instant of time that a man needs to harden his resolution. Then Harlaw said: "In yonder." He pointed to the door.

"Open it up," commanded Birch.

Harlaw turned the key in the lock and stepped back.

"You do the opening for yourself, will you?" he invited. "I don't like teeth with poison on 'em."

Little Willie Birch stepped undaunted to the door. "Who left the dog with you?"

"Gent by name of Dugan, or Newman, or something like

that. I didn't get it very good," answered Harlaw.

"Oh, you didn't get it very good, eh?" asked Birch with meaning. He laid his hand on the knob of the door as he spoke.

"I wouldn't walk in on no mad dog . . . not in a small room," suggested Oliver rather loudly. He guessed that his voice might have an effect on the Masterman, but he was unprepared for the influence of those added days of separation.

A thunderbolt struck the door that Birch had started to open, slamming it shut with a crash. It was a howling, snarling, growling thunderbolt that shook the house, and the assembled men heard the claws ripping and mangling the door from the inside.

Birch, for an instant, hesitated, then he turned suddenly and shrugged his shoulders.

"All right," he said. "It's a mad dog, I guess. You better get your friend Newman or Dugan to take a look at it, Harlaw."

"I'll take a look at the fool dog myself, pretty quick," said Harlaw. "I ain't gonna have a decent house wrecked."

They left the place, and, as they went, the eyes of Oliver found those of Harlaw for a brief instant with more than words could have uttered.

In the street, Birch went on frankly: "I maybe've got a wrong steer, Deacon . . . if that's your name. We'll go along and have a look at the jail."

The jail door was opened to them by Bud.

One side of his face was swollen and purple from the effects of the blow of the night before, so that he had to talk from the side of his mouth.

"Know this fellow, Bud?" asked Birch.

The jailer scanned Oliver with indifference.

"You mean, is he the guy that socked me?"

"Well, look him over."

Bud stepped closer, and with a glance measured his man. "Him? Why, he ain't a quarter the size. That Oliver, he's a *man!* Look . . . when he socked me, it was like the big knobs of a walkin' beam had poked me in the face. I stopped thinkin'. I just done a flop. Now this here. . . ." He made a gesture that dismissed Oliver to the ranks of ordinary men.

"You know Baldy Wendell?" asked Birch.

"Yeah! Now, there's something like! Funny I didn't think of Baldy Wendell before. He might've. . . ."

"Not that I'd wanna be refreshin' your memory too much, Bud, but this very man here picked Baldy up and threw him in a corner, and then knocked him out as cold as the nails in your shoe. Take a look at the sound of his voice, too, while you're about it."

"Look me all over," agreed Oliver carelessly, and he laughed a little as he said it.

Bud narrowed his eyes, and canted his head to one side. "He put Baldy down, did he?" pondered Bud. "Well, that's all right, too. But he ain't the boy that plastered me."

"Where's Jennings?" demanded Birch.

"Hey, Jennings!" called Bud.

Jennings came with a slow step. His face was pale and rather set; in his eyes there was a look of gloomy defiance.

"How about our friend, here?" asked Birch. "Ever hear his voice before?"

Jennings looked at them sullenly.

"Ever meet me before?" said Oliver, as though submitting willingly to the test.

Jennings put back his head with a slight jerk, and looked fairly into the eyes of the taller man. There was no question in the mind of Oliver; he had been recognized. He waited, tense as a cat, for the single word that would condemn him. Then a faint shadow passed over the face of Jennings. "No," he said. "I never laid eyes on him before."

"Wait a minute," broke in Birch. "A man in a parka, he looks a good pile bigger than in togs like these. Suppose he was in a parka, and wore a mask over his face . . . ?"

Jennings shook his head. "I know," he replied. "You couldn't fool me. I'd know any whisper of his voice, if I heard him speak, clean across a room. I'd be sure to know." He nodded as he spoke.

Riley Oliver was staggered with amazement.

"All right," said Birch. "That's that. I've brought you a bit out of your way, Deacon. The drinks are on me. Come and get 'em."

They left the jail and entered a bar. Birch grew talkative.

"What I mean," he remarked, "when I saw how easily you took everything, Deacon, I says to myself that we sure had the right man. You didn't talk much. You seemed easy. I says to myself that nobody has that much nerve, unless he's a master mind. You know what I mean? Here's in your eye . . . and hopin' that I never run into the bunch of fives that put a new face on Baldy. What a sock *he* got!"

They drank together.

"In town long?" asked Birch.

"I don't know," said Oliver. "I'm waiting, and soaking up the easy time. That's all."

"Sorry I dragged you out, partner."

"Why, that's all right. I'm not mad. I'm flattered."

He went back to the hotel, and a volley of questions stopped him in the lobby.

"He thought I was Oliver! What a chance!" he said, and went upstairs.

But in his own room, as he lighted the lamp, he was so absent-minded that he allowed the flame of the match to singe his fingertips. He was remembering the wistful, rather hungry eyes of Willie Birch as the trail-man bade him good night.

But Jennings was the chief miracle. Why had the man refused to name him and turn him over to the law? Clearly, recognition had been in the jailer's eyes, and yet he had failed to speak. It was so mysterious that Oliver's brain grew dizzy in the contemplation of the puzzle.

Then he went to sleep, remembering Christy's dubious and rather frightened face. The most extraordinary part of that strange affair was that Christy had *not* recognized the voice of Oliver.

Chapter Sixteen

HAWKS—NORTH OR SOUTH

On that unfortunate spring, winter closed down again. Before Oliver fell asleep, he heard the shriek of the blizzard that fell upon Fairbanks from the north, and all through the night the thrusting lance-points of the cold found him, here and there, and kept him turning in his bed. The same cold wind would be arresting the thaw everywhere, turning the half-melted snow crisp again, first clouding the running rivulets, then frosting them to solid ice, with the ripples of their swift flowing engraved in their depths. It contented him more, in his sleep, to be aware of the storm and of winter's return, for this climate seemed, in a way, to bring him back to what had been his country for nine years.

He was between sleep and waking, when a voice roused him completely. He sat up with a movement that brought a revolver from under his pillow and into his hand, pointing toward a dim figure that stood between him and the half-light of dawn that filled the windows.

"Quietly, my brother," said this soft voice that had entered his dream.

Riley Oliver steadied his head.

"I am not from Willie Birch," said the stranger.

Now, as his eyes began to penetrate the gloom more easily, Oliver was able to see that both the other's hands were empty; in shame he put aside his gun.

"Who from?" he asked.

"Not from a newspaper, either," said the other.

"Let's have a light, then," suggested the big man.

He was conscious of his own great size as he measured the below average inches of the man near the window.

"We can talk better in the dark . . . the sort of talking I want to do," replied the visitor.

"Well?" said Oliver.

"I'm Jap Laforge."

A chill that was not from the wind went up the back of Oliver's neck.

"All right, Jap," he said.

"Dropped in for a chat," said Laforge.

As though the light were on, as though his host were inviting him, he sat down beside the little center table, took out a cigarette, lighted it, and sent a wave of thin, rather sickeningly sweet tobacco smoke toward the other.

In the flare of the match, Oliver had seen nothing except the lowered hood of the parka. "How's everything?" asked Oliver, vaguely fumbling for words and ideas, for all he could think of was the description of the blood-curdling crimes of Jap Laforge that he had heard in the past. All of the blood that had been shed in them was cold blood, for it appeared that mercy did not exist in this man.

His question was not answered. Laforge merely said: "We might do something together, Oliver."

"That's a queer name to call me," said Oliver. "My name's Sam Deacon."

"That goes with me. Only . . . one of my men saw you work with Baldy Wendell."

"What man?"

"Nobody you'd know likely. But call yourself any name you care to, Oliver. You and I could do business together."

"Maybe."

"Depends on your attitude."

"About what?"

"Me. What do you think of me, brother?"

"I wonder why you waste your time up here."

"Waste it?"

"Yes. Up here in Alaska. With your brains and your system, you could make money in far warmer places than this, Jap."

"Hell, for instance?"

"Not as far south as that, either. But I don't see what attracts you up here."

"You mean, more stuff for me to get other places?"

"Yes. That and other things, I mean." He was surprised by the ease with which he found words.

"You've seen hawks sailing by the Río Grande, haven't you?" asked Jap Laforge.

"Yes, of course."

"They don't need many feathers down there, eh?"

"No."

"You've seen the big white hawks and the eagles up north, too?"

"Yes."

"They have more feathers?"

"Of course."

"But which hawk is most happy . . . the southern one or the northern one?"

"I see what you mean. The cold doesn't bother a bird that knows his business."

"I thought you might understand. I thought, besides, that I might be able to show you the way to the good times, up here in the north."

"What steered you my way?"

"Christy."

"Christy?"

"He's one of my boys."

"Christy is?"

"Yes."

"That surprises me a good deal."

"He's a bright fellow."

"Yes. He's bright."

"Not your style?"

"Not quite."

"The fact is, Oliver, I don't care what you do to Christy after the job is finished. I never care what any of my men do to one another, after the job on hand is finished. I've said the same thing to Christy . . . I say it to them all."

"That's clear, then."

"I hope so. Now, what about yourself?"

"You seem to know a lot about me."

"I know a good bit."

"Well, fire ahead."

"What are you doing here?"

"Can't you guess that?"

"Trying to get Melville out of jail. But why?"

At this question, Oliver had to pause, to consider.

"Don't say that it's because he's your friend," suggested Laforge. "I hate a hypocrite worse than I hate all hell." There was warmth in his voice as well as in his words.

"What can I say, then?"

"Say the truth."

"You'd better prompt me, Laforge."

"Say it's because you want Melville's girl. I don't wonder. She's a beauty."

"You've seen her?"

"Of course. She's a pretty thing. One of the neatest. You want her. Get her father out of the can, and you'll have her for yourself . . . dead easy. Is that right?"

"That may be the idea," said Oliver almost dreamily.

"It's idea enough to start a fellow like you. Though I must say that it's damned cool, the way you've walked into this town and sat down in it."

"Thanks."

"If it's a fact that they want you for a killing on the Río Grande, that is."

"Christy tell you that?"

"I never could understand how you and Melville happened to talk so freely to Christy."

"I never thought that he'd live to tell other people about what we said."

"Why didn't you crack him over the head and bury him deeper than the summer thaw?"

"I had other ideas. I like to hear a rat squeal when he's killed."

Jap Laforge laughed gently, tenderly. "I know what you mean when you say that," he declared. "I know exactly what you mean!"

He laughed again, and the brooding tenderness of the sound took Oliver's breath.

"Only," said Laforge, "it was a great mistake! You might have known he'd slip away from Melville."

"Yes, it was a mistake, of course."

"Now you want to get Melville out?"

"Yes."

"I can do that for you. I can produce him any time of the night . . . I almost said any time of the day or the night."

"How?"

"Parlor magic, that's all."

"And what do I pay?"

"An hour or two of your time."

"For what?"

"For Willie Birch."

"You mean, to snag him?"

"Not just to leave cards. . . . No, I didn't mean just to make a little social call."

Oliver found that a shudder was creeping through his very heart. And for the first time in his life he discovered that his antipathy toward this scoundrel was not aggressive; he loathed the man, but he had no immediate wish to do anything about it. Was it fear that locked up his powers of will and of action? That consideration thawed his reserve at once.

"I've got to tell you something, Jap," he said.

"Go ahead."

"The only man I ever killed in all my days was a double-crossing hound of a sneaking hypocrite. And now I want to kill another."

"Christy?"

"Yes . . . and Laforge."

"Something told me it might turn out this way," remarked Laforge calmly. He stood up and yawned, stretching both hands high above his head. He added: "But since you're this way, I can depend on the chivalrous gentleman who never lifts a hand against his guest, eh?" He dropped his arms, and sighed. The cigarette he spat from his lips, and ground it with his heel into the matting.

"We'd better have some light," said Laforge. "This may take a little more time than I thought." He leaned over the table and pulled up the chimney of the lamp. The glass screeched softly against the metal guards, then a match spurted light that spilled wildly over the face and hand of Laforge, without revealing more than a few gleaming surfaces. The flame touched the wick, ran across it, leaped high, and steadied again when the chimney was pressed back into place.

"You've never seen me before. And there are no pictures

except those that liars have drawn of me. You'll want a look . . . so take a good one." So said Laforge, as he lifted the lamp and held it beside his face. He went on talking, interrupting himself with little pauses, telling Riley Oliver what to look at, then giving him a moment in which to observe what had been pointed out. He sounded like a conscientious guide in a picture gallery.

"Notice, first, the Oriental type . . . the broad cheekbones, slant eyes, wide mouth, and the yellow skin, fitted smoothly and closely. Fitted so close that it will be hard for time to wrinkle it. The added interest is in knowing that Jap Laforge is *not* a Jap at all, and that he hasn't a drop of Oriental blood in his veins. Observe that the eyes rarely seem open, but that they are always bright . . . an animal brightness, you might say. Here the cruelty of the man appears . . . and in the width of the mouth and the muscular thickness of the lips.

"Now for the profile, which shows you the chin of a man who never surrenders a purpose. There is an outthrust of the mouth that means a brutal desire for physical pleasure. The nose is blunt and wide, yet it has a slightly Semitic downward curve in it. Now we climb to the forehead, and you will observe here the last chapter of the man, built up in a lofty tower, squared out at the sides, and bulging in the center. A good brain could be packed away there, and you will recall, of course, that this fellow never has been defeated in any of his important schemes.

"Again, we consider the full face. We remark that there seems to be a frown between the eyes, although no wrinkles of frowning are actually written into the skin. It is the Jovian cloud, perhaps. And now we finish with an identifying mark, a signature on the portrait, as it were."

He tilted his head far back, suddenly, and, holding the lamp close to his throat, showed a vast, jagged white scar that shone as though it had been freshly painted in with silver paint. It ran straight across the neck, disappearing around the corners of the jaws. It was inconceivable that a cut so wide and so long could have done less than take off the entire head. Jap Laforge brought his head erect again. "And so we conclude . . . with many thanks," he said. He smiled, with his half-closed eyes above the light of the lamp. The corners of his mouth angled upward in that smile, and the light of it slanted up in his eyes, also.

He put the lamp back on the table. "Now we know each other better," he said.

Riley Oliver got an impression of wide shoulders, smoothly padded out with power; of arms like a monkey's; of a body like a monkey's, also, pinched in at the waist. But these things did not matter. The world knew well enough that the great Laforge concentrated enormous strength in a comparatively small compass, and that he was a traveler swift enough to escape even from the rapid wing of Willie Birch. But nothing about his physical status mattered. It was the face that counted, because it hinted at the qualities of the mind behind it.

Riley Oliver, feeling strangely dazed and confused, was glad when he was no longer forced to stare at the brilliantly lighted horror of that face. Now that the lamp was back on the table, the face could be seen clearly enough, but shadows, mercifully, made the smile seem to be real and made the eyes at times seem to gleam with something that resembled human sympathy and amusement.

Riley Oliver felt the working of a spell. Men said that this creature before him was a mighty hypnotist. Certainly he made all others conform to his will. And so a fine sweat broke out on Oliver's body, and he stood up suddenly.

"What do you want, Laforge?" he asked.

"You don't have to stand up to fight me," said Laforge. "You can sit down."

"I'll keep standing," answered Oliver.

"You don't mind if I keep to my chair, then? Of course, there's no cause for any alarm on your part. I'm in your hands. I'm here, inside your room, and you have a gun in your hand. A gun like yours, in a hand like yours, never misses at this distance . . . not if it is shooting at a snipe in the wind. I'm absolutely in your hands."

"Go on," said Oliver. "Say your say, and then get out of my room, will you?"

"Why, man," answered Laforge, "you see the importance of the things that I'm pointing out to you, don't you? Here I am, in your power. And if you put a bullet through my heart or head all your own sins will be forgiven. They'll no longer want you for murder, down there in San Marco of the Bells. . . . I've heard those bells, by the way. . . . Pull the trigger of that gun, and you're free to go where you please in the world. All the old sins will be forgiven. Yes, and people will respect you, and look up to you all the rest of your days."

"Damn you," muttered Oliver. "You know I won't shoot a man till his hand is filled. And you're in my room."

"Your room is your house, and your house is sacred," interpreted Laforge.

"I've asked you before, I'm asking you again . . . tell me what you want, and then get out . . . or I'll throw you out, Laforge."

Laforge leaned forward in his chair so that his face came into shadow, out of which the eyes and the teeth shone. "I wonder if you could do that?" he pondered, speaking gently.

"I think I can," said Riley Oliver.

"Yes, I think you could, too," agreed Laforge.

"So tell me what brought you here . . . then get."

"I want an honest man," said Laforge. "That's what brought me here. I'm tired of crooks, and I want an honest man."

The breath was taken from Oliver.

"Something about the way you met two men like Christy and Birch, for the sake of your friend Melville, shows me that at last I've met what I've heard about . . . an honest man. I've heard about that freak of nature all my life. And the way you hunted the pair of them through the mountains was another thing that warmed my heart. All for the bank robber, Melville. It made me decide to have you."

"Did it?"

"Yes. You're hardening yourself in resistance, but that's useless. I've decided to have you on my side . . . and I'll get you."

"How?"

"I'll buy you."

"Plenty of money, eh?"

"Money? I'm not such a fool. I'll buy you with the sort of coin that you value. I'll deliver Bob Melville into your hands, Oliver."

"My name is Sam Deacon. You're talking like a fool."

"No, old son. I know what Oliver can do, and I know what you've done. You could pull the wool over Christy's eyes. That fool! But I know there can't be two men in Alaska capable of doing what you and Oliver can do. Therefore, you're Oliver."

This quiet logic crushed some of Riley Oliver's resistance. He began to feel that his mind was as a child's mind, compared with that of this great criminal. The fear that had been in him from the first now increased rapidly, and the sense of fear was utterly new to him. It took the blood of strength out of his very soul.

"I'll deliver your friend Melville from the jail," Laforge went on. "I know ways of doing it. I'll give him to you safe and sound . . . and then your position will be perfect. When you bring the girl to her father, and when she falls into his arms, Riley, think how they'll worship you! She'd follow you around the world on her hands and knees. I give you the father, Riley, and I give you the daughter. Now think it over."

Oliver went to the table, rested his trembling hands on the edge of it, and stared down into the eyes of Laforge. In those eyes he seemed to see his alternative fates, clearly expressed. Either he did this thing and was rewarded with a glorious love and happiness, or else he became a hounded creature that the law would hang, at last, thereby living in the girl's mind as no more than a memory—an unsavory memory, at that.

He wanted to fight against this temptation by staring at Laforge's face, realizing its ugliness, contemplating the history of Laforge's crimes. But the soothing voice of his visitor went on: "I wouldn't use you often, either. Perhaps once a year, when I need a man for perfect trust in a great job. I'd arrange everything, so that you could fade out of your home with a good excuse . . . a hunting trip or something like that. And I'd return you safe and sound, to wait till the next year came around. . . . Understand my plan? My hands have been tied. I've had to work alone most of the time, in every big deal, simply because the tools I've had my hands on have been made of bad metal. But with you, Oliver, I could chisel open the heart of the world . . . and take out the gold." He laughed softly, fiercely. "It wouldn't last forever, either. One or two jobs . . . maybe three . . . and we'd have enough to make us all wealthy forever. And then you fade out into the world, and I go to a certain place in the South Seas that I know the savor of. I've had the taste of it in my brain all these years. . . . Happiness, my boy! That's what I'm offering. And a chance to serve the people you love . . . Bob Melville, and you can marry the girl. Yes, by heaven, and cover her with pearls and wrap her in velvets!"

Riley Oliver put back his head and groaned.

"If you're the man I take you for, you'll do it," said Laforge. "Or are you rat enough to think only about yourself? Afraid to dirty your hands for the sake of Melville and the girl? I'm offering you the only chance you'll have. You know that you'll never be able to get inside the jail again, to free Melville. I'm the only power in the world that can put him in your hands. And remember, Oliver . . . you don't have to start paying me until I've delivered the goods."

"I've got to think. I can't think while I'm strangling," said Oliver in a low voice. "Come back tomorrow night by this time, and I'll answer you."

"You're throwing away chances if you wait. You're suspected now. By tomorrow night you'll probably be grabbed. Be a man, and make up your mind on the spot."

"Just one day!" groaned Riley Oliver. "Give me one day, and then come back again."

He closed his eyes for a long moment. The thought of the girl and the picture of her made him look out suddenly, again, and he found that he was alone. The great Laforge had vanished as soundlessly as he had come.

Chapter Seventeen

WITH KNIVES

Oliver took himself in hand as though his body were a slave and his will its master. In his early years in the wilderness there had been times when he had had to struggle with himself for hours and days, fighting hard to keep loneliness from driving him mad. But that school had taught him will power, and had hammered and tempered it until it was the true working engine. So now he lay in his bed and beat down and conquered, first, the jumping of his nerves, then the quivering of his muscles. The dread of Laforge he drew from his mind and cast out. Lastly, he erased the face of the girl, looked for a moment into blankness, and then fell asleep.

It was the first full sleep he had had since he had taken the trail from Candy Creek. When he wakened in the morning, his mind was buzzing with the last voices that had spoken in his dreams, and as his brain cleared he knew that he had come to a decision. The payment that Laforge had offered was too high to be rejected. Not only too high for Riley Oliver's sake, but too high for the girl's and her father's. He would accept the terms that night, when Laforge came again to his room—as he surely *would* come.

In the meantime, there was another day to get through, and he felt that his footing in Fairbanks was as unsure as though he were walking on quicksand. At any moment the danger of the law might seize him by the heel and draw him under.

He dressed, went down to breakfast, and found Bob

Melville's daughter in the dining room. Twenty pairs of eyes lifted instantly, and began to travel back and forth between them. After all, it was not a small affront that she apparently had given him the night before, when they had encountered each other in the upper hall, under the eyes of Birch and Christy.

He felt that something was demanded of him, so he went straight up to her chair. She was smiling faintly, a habit that pretty women have at all times, as though they feel it their duty to make the most of what God has given them. But as he came up, the smile vanished, and she opened her eyes at him. It was a very good simulation of fear. Two or three chairs were pushed back, as though some of the other men actually feared that Oliver might do her an injury.

He said, loudly: "You bore down on me pretty hard last night. Give me a fair break and let me talk to you sometime, will you? I want to show you that I'm no man-eater!"

"I think I may have said something ugly," said the girl. "I'd be glad to talk with you at any time, Mister Deacon, and I'm sorry. . . ."

"Oh, it's all right," said Oliver.

He left her abruptly, and sat down at a small table, his back to her. Other people were muttering together. Chairs that had been pushed back were drawn forward again. And contentment grew in the heart of Oliver, for he knew that he had paved the way that would lead to another interview with the girl. People would not suspect their intimacy, after this breaking of the ground. Otherwise, their conversations might awaken the old suspicion that he was indeed Riley Oliver, and her father's friend.

A man entered the room and paused beside his table. It was Jennings, the jailer, looking more like a bulldog than ever. He seemed to have a paler skin and bigger pouches under his eyes.

"Mind if I take this chair?" asked Jennings.

"Help yourself," answered Oliver.

A voice called across the room, "Hey, Jennings, this your day off?"

"I'm gonna taste something besides pork and beans," said Jennings. "The kind of a cook that they got at the jail is a tramp, what I mean to say."

"No more funny business from Oliver, eh?" asked another man.

"The next funny business out of him is gonna be the last!" declared Jennings. He leaned a little forward, resting his elbows on the edge of the table, after he had given his order to the waitress. And he said: "This is my day off, Oliver."

"Put that name out of sight, will you?" asked Riley Oliver.

"I'm talking soft," answered Jennings. "I was just saying that this is my day off."

"Going to spend it with me, brother?"

"It's the last day for one of us," said Jennings ominously.

Oliver took a good swallow of coffee and over the brim of the cup marked his companion well. On either side of Jennings's mouth there was a white streak. His jaw was moving in and out a trifle.

"I don't know about its being the last day," said Oliver.

Outside the wind rose suddenly, fell on the hotel and, for an instant, shook it with an angry hand.

"I can show you up," declared Jennings, "and I'll do, it if you won't play my game, my way. I knew you, when they brought you around to the jail. I knew you like a brother. I could have hooked you then, but it wasn't my way of playing the game."

"Go on," urged Oliver. "Something's eating you."

"Yeah, something is. The other night I was off my feed. You got the drop on me . . . and I showed yellow." The two white streaks widened into large patches in the man's cheeks.

"You were all right," answered Oliver. "I tried a mean line with you. I had to get somewhere, and get there pretty fast."

"You broke me down," said Jennings. "Now I'm gonna break you."

"Break me?"

"Yeah. You're gonna play my game, and you're gonna play it my way."

"Maybe I am. What's the idea?"

"What you started in the jail we're gonna fight out now."

"Fight with what?"

"You're better with a gun than I am, maybe . . . and you're too big and hard for me to tackle with my hands. But how do you work with a knife, brother?"

Oliver squinted suddenly at him. "You been in Mexico?"

"Yeah. I've been in Mexico and watched them at it."

"So have I," said Oliver.

"A pair of hunting knives would be good enough," said Jennings, while his eyes traveled over Oliver's big body with a cold and lasting hate.

"You want us to go somewhere and carve each other, do you?"

"It's that, or else I bawl you out. Take it any way you want."

"If I win, I leave a big red spot behind me, and that's bad news. Ought to be something more in the pot than that."

"What else? You can't back down out of this. You work with me, or I'll tell Birch who you are."

Jennings's lips twisted, showing his teeth. One of them was broken off short. "Are you a yellow hound?" he asked. His voice trembled a little, and the uncertainty in his eyes proved that he was not altogether sure of himself. "Do I have to *buy* a fight with you, to square myself?"

He wanted to vindicate his own pride in himself—for that was patently his purpose—to wipe out the shame of his surrender in the jail. Now he was ready to die for it. Already the berserker madness gleamed in his pale eyes.

A new hope came suddenly to Riley Oliver. Here was a means by which he might avoid that terrible alliance which Jap Laforge had offered to him. He said: "Get this straight, Jennings. You want to fight it out with me. Guns or bare hands are my medicine, but you want knives. Well, what do I get out of it?"

"What do you want?" asked Jennings.

"This is your day off."

"Well, what of that?"

"There's more than one set of keys to the jail."

"Hold on! What are you driving at, Oliver?"

Riley Oliver glanced casually around the room, and saw that no one was marking them. "If you win, I'm dead, Jennings. That right?"

"Aye. It'll be to a finish," said Jennings.

"Well?"

"After you're dead, would it matter to you that I had the keys to the jail?"

"I see what you mean. If you manage to cut my throat, you get the jail keys off me . . . ? You poor fool, would you try to go back into the jail another time?"

"I'd try, maybe."

A grin, half-contemptuous and half-admiring, set the mouth of Jennings twitching. "If I can show you the keys, you'll fight it out fair and square with me, Oliver?"

"I'll do that."

"When?"

"This evening, about the end of the strong light."

Jennings pushed back his chair. "Where, Oliver?"

"On the edge of town . . . say on the road to the lake."

"I'll be there." Jennings arose suddenly, triumph in his face.

"You've ordered a meal," said Oliver. "Better sit down and eat it."

"The devil with the food! I'll pay, but the devil with it."

"If you walk out like that, people may start talking. We don't want them to notice anything strange, do we?"

Reluctantly, Jennings sat down again. The waitress came, loaded with heavy crockery, and Jennings began to make vague passes at his food. But Oliver saw that his hands were trembling.

"I'll bring two Bowie knives, so the blades'll be the same length. And before the finish. . . ." He failed to finish the sentence. He showed his teeth again, in something that was not a smile.

"This evening," said Oliver, "at the head of the lake road. . . . So long till then."

"So long," answered Jennings. He had the look of a dog on a leash that marks its prey and will return to it when freedom comes.

Oliver went out of the room with a strange, hollow sense of weakness in his breast.

It was better this way than to become the partner of the terrible Laforge, but he was afraid—he was horribly afraid.

Chapter Eighteen

A FAREWELL

The fight with Baldy and the suspicions which Birch and Christy had thrown upon Riley Oliver had made Oliver a marked man in Fairbanks. There were a dozen men in the hotel who would have been glad to buy his liquor for that day, and they as much as said so, clustering around him.

When he smiled and denied them, a cluster still adhered as he passed out into the street. He faced the wind, and the weight of it soon scoured away the hangers-on, long before he came to the place of Harlaw the Dane. That fellow pursed his mouth and squinted his eyes as though Riley Oliver were very bad news, indeed. Then they stepped into the lee of a shed. The storm arched over them like the spray of a cataract, but they were in comparative peace behind their shelter.

"You want something. You got a hungry look, brother," said Harlaw, grinning. "I hear you been beating up some of the boys, eh? Oh, man, but I wish you'd slammed Wendell just once more. He had it coming to him. I used a pick handle on him once, but the hickory didn't do as much as your fists, I guess."

"I want some dogs," said Riley Oliver. "I want the five best dogs that you can lay your hands on."

"That's about fifteen hundred dollars," said Harlaw the Dane.

"If I manage the job I've got on hand, I'll be able to pay you double that. If I can't manage it . . . you get the dogs back."

"It's a hard wind," said Harlaw the Dane. "It's a mean, cold wind, too, for this time of the year."

"It'll let up and the spring thaw'll come any minute."

"You got what kind of a job on hand?"

"If you really want to know, I'll tell you all about it."

Harlaw chewed hard on his nether lip. "No, I don't want to know," he said. "But I'll tell you this . . . if it's another go at the jail, they'll eat you. They've put on a double guard."

"Have they? On account of me?"

"Kind of warms your heart, does it?"

"I'm a simple sort of *hombre,*" declared Riley Oliver. "You'll build that team for me?"

"I'll build it . . . and wait with it where?"

"Have it in front of the Pembroke Saloon."

"That's pretty near the jail, eh?"

"Never mind what you're thinking, Harlaw. Will you do what I say?"

"Yeah. I'll do it." He started to speak again, but an eddy of the wind thrust into his mouth and gagged him.

"It's fixed, then?" demanded Oliver.

"Yeah. I'll furnish the team . . . the best I can get in Fairbanks."

"I'll need the best on the trail I run, all right."

"Yeah," growled Harlaw. "I know. Wings would likely be the real article for you . . . on the trail that *you'll* run. But I'll have the dogs ready in time, and I'll have 'em at the Pembroke place whenever you say."

"This evening, after the sun goes down."

"Are you going to stay around Fairbanks as long as that?"

"Why not?"

"Birch came back here, full of questions about you. Talked a lot. He didn't ask about the mad dog. But hell, Oliver, I thought it was all a bust, till you spoke and that

Husky started goin' crazy to get at you. I thought it was all a bust, but you come through at the finish. Luck . . . that's what saved us. But Birch ain't through. He's been back here and askin' me a lot of questions about you. He still suspects something. He's a regular bloodhound, and it's blood that he wants in this deal."

"You'll have a chance to see him today. Tell him that Jap Laforge is in town. That may take his mind off me a little."

"He wouldn't be bothered by hearing that. He knows that even Laforge ain't man enough to come into Fairbanks."

"It's a fact, though . . . I've seen him."

"Are you with Laforge?" asked the Dane harshly.

"That once is the only time I've seen him."

"If I'm wrong about you . . . ," mused Harlaw the Dane. "If you ain't a straight crook, after all. . . ."

Harlaw held in his hand a short club with a padded leather head. Those who have seen wild dogs "broken" for sled work will understand what the ordinary use of that tool was. Now, as a savage thought worked into Harlaw's brain, the head of the club rose and fell as he flexed his powerful hand.

This fellow, in both looks and nature, would make a fit blood-brother and companion for Jennings, thought Oliver. He admired them both. Both were worthy, and both terrible because of a certain headlong, brutal honesty of soul.

"You're not wrong," said Oliver. "Even if I die, you'll be paid every penny of the hard cash I owe you. But that isn't what's important. If I live to have sons and grandsons, and then a couple more generations were added on, every man jack of 'em will have to hear about a Dane called Harlaw."

"Aw, that's a lot of bunk," said Harlaw. "Aw, get out of here, will you? I'll have the team lined up in front of Pembroke's saloon, all right, this evening. . . . Go on and run along, now! Gonna try to pull my leg for something else?"

Oliver grinned at him, and straightway started back for the hotel. It was harder to walk before the wind than it had been to struggle against it, for he was compelled to lean far back. Even the pressure was apt to skate his feet over the frozen surface.

At the hotel, he walked through the lobby without pause, returned to his room, and stretched out on the bed, for he would need all of the strength that rest might give to him.

The windows in the old structure were rattling like tin pans, but that noise and the wolfish howling of the storm troubled him less than did occasional footfalls that stamped up the stairs and down the hall. For each time they approached he told himself that the men of the law were upon him.

No matter how his adventure with Jennings turned out, he already had determined to have nothing to do with Laforge. And perhaps that cunning devil with the yellow skin and the slanted eyes was guessing that conclusion, and was ready to act against Riley Oliver. He would not be taken alive while there were bullets in his gun, although sometimes it seemed to him that it would be worthwhile to hear the bells of San Marco, down on the Texas border, even if he were to hang on the day of his return. However, he began to feel that no matter where he remained during the rest of the day, the hotel was the worst of places. At that very moment a hand tapped lightly at his door.

He was off the bed and across the floor in an instant, his mind resolved. It was only strange that Birch should give him the warning before rushing into the room; his own part must be to tear the door open and charge straight out upon the men who perhaps were waiting stealthily there in the hall.

He drew his Colt, weighed it once in his hand, and then jerked the door wide—to find the small form of Mary Melville standing on the threshold. He could barely check himself and step suddenly back.

She looked from his face to the gun, and back again, then she stepped inside and closed the door behind her.

"I thought somebody else . . . ," he began.

"This morning, at breakfast, when you spoke, I knew it was because you wanted to talk to me again. I've only waited till you came back."

"You shouldn't have come into my room. You'd better get out now."

"No one saw me. And there'll be no more danger of them seeing me go. I want to ask you about the man who sat at your table. People tell me that he is Jennings, the jailer. Is that true?"

"Yes, that's Jennings."

"He was trying to control his expression," Mary said, "but I could read something under the surface. I kept watching him, and it was like seeing some horrible, nightmarish creature glide up through shadowy water. The thing kept getting nearer and nearer to the surface, yet never quite arrived."

"D'you think that other people thought the same thing when they watched him?" asked Oliver sharply.

"No. If I hadn't cared, myself, I don't suppose I would have noticed anything, either. One needed a clue, so to speak."

What she said about "caring"—that was a clue that Riley Oliver would have been glad to develop for a moment, but he realized that there were things which he must never say to her. No one so shut away in the outer night of chance had any right to speak to such a woman as this, opening his heart.

She added: "Will you tell me what he was saying to you?"

"Tell you what he was talking about?"

"Yes. I'd like to know."

"No. I can't tell you a word."

A smile came and went like an apology on her face. "I shouldn't ask after your business."

"Jennings is a chapter that I can't tell about. That's all."

"Will you tell me what you wanted to talk about today?"

He fumbled for words again, found none, and could only stare. If only she would sit down, then he could be seated, also, and that would make everything easier. But she continued to stand at the door, with her hands behind her back.

It was but a dull sifting of light that came through the sleeted window panes, but he could see her well enough. He would be able to see her with his eyes closed—and all his life. It seemed that his silence began to give him an advantage and a power over her. It made her nervous.

"If you won't talk, I'll tell you what is on my own mind," she said.

"I'd like to hear it," he answered simply.

"Even if you get farther away, they will follow and run you down. There is nothing mystic about me, but somehow I seem to feel the bullets striking you. The first time I saw you, I knew that you couldn't last long."

"Why?"

"Because you were different . . . and men will kill you just because of the difference."

"Did your father tell you that?"

"No. He loves you. He told me that God never made a finer man, or a truer friend, or a greater heart. And I believe him. I'm begging you to give up the hope of making that rescue at the jail . . . because if you do try it, I know that they'll follow till they kill you. I know it as surely as I hear the wind howl."

"What shall I do, according to you?"

"Give all this up because it's impossible."

"And after I give up this game . . . then what?"

"You made a beautiful life for yourself before. My father says that you made the whole wilderness your yard and garden . . . that you can call the wild geese out of the sky . . . that you know every sound and every sign of the animals."

"There were nine years of that . . . but they came to an end," he told her.

"Why?"

"When I talked with you. . . . That ended the old life."

"Is that it? Am I in your head?"

That question was as painful to him as the slow passing of a dull knife through his flesh, but he answered: "I've said so, and I'll stick to it, I suppose."

"Because," she went on, as though he had not spoken the last words at all, "at first I thought it was because Father loves you. . . . Then I knew it was something else that kept pressing the thought of you right against my brain."

He left the window and got halfway across the room, where he stopped like a witless thing that did not know how to get around the table that was in his path.

"You'd better be going on. It's no good saying things like this," he told her.

"It's a lot of good. You go somewhere into the back country, and wait. I'll stand by Father until the trial is finished . . . and I know that the law won't be so savage as we think, or so blind. The truth will come out, somehow. He'll be free, and then I'll come back to you."

He got around the table and stood over her. "I suppose it's because you're so far north and haven't seen much of other men for a while," he said, "but I won't say it or think it. I'm going to believe everything. . . . Look! If I could put the world in my pocket, I wouldn't have it in exchange for you. But all the same, talking's no good. If there were ten of you, you couldn't stop me from trying my luck to get your father free. He'd have a chance against the law, except for Christy. But Christy's alive, and free, and against him . . . and Christy's a devil. All we can do is to say good bye."

"I knew that I couldn't stop you, and I had to try. I knew I couldn't stop you. God wouldn't give me that much happiness! Does it have to be good bye . . . right now?"

"Right now."

She held up her arms to him. He was both awkward and afraid. Still he had to explain as he bent over her: "All these years, he's been one half of my world, and I've been one half of his. If I gave up trying for him now, I'd be too cheap and mean to get into hell, even."

"I knew I couldn't stop you," she said. Her body began to tremble against him, and his heart turned hollow with misery. "I don't suppose I even want to stop you. But all in a moment to feel that you love me, and then to say good bye forever. . . ."

"Stop crying!" he commanded.

"I shall."

"Now go back to your room."

He simply opened the door, and she went past him down the hall, turned once so that he saw her tear-wet face as it smiled at him, then she was gone.

He closed the door again, and heard a voice saying: "That's all right . . . that's over." But it was his own voice.

Life seemed to be over, too, except for the brief, red trail that now lay before him. The injustice of the world had made for him a nine-year desert, only that this moment might bloom in it and make all well.

He stood blindly in the little room, and he was still standing there a long time later, when through his coma came the frantic howl of a wolf—or of a wolfish dog. Then there was the rattle of nails as the brute galloped down the hall toward his room. He recognized the note of the Masterman.

Chapter Nineteen

BLOWING THE BANK

The big dog slid to a halt with another howl, outside of the door to his room, as Oliver hurried to meet him. Whatever had happened, Harlaw had not betrayed him, he was sure, but perhaps it meant that while the Dane was mushing the dog team toward the lake, Birch or his men had searched the yards of the kennel man again, and had finally located Masterman—located him—turned him loose on a lead—let him take them on a leash, with that inevitable sureness of scent that could follow a trail inches deep in snow, straight to his master. Having found Oliver's dog, they would be able to let the beast show them the way to his owner, and so begin a trail that could have no ending except far away in the southland, at San Marco of the Bells.

It seemed to Oliver a perfect and a cruel treachery to make the dog betray him in this manner. Instantly, he was out in the hall, where the Masterman towered in the gloom at him in ecstatic recognition. He struck the leaping body with a gesture, and saw two running figures loom at the head of the stairs.

He wanted to take them by the throat, but he was not in the wilderness snow. He was in the dangerous jungle of humanity, and he would have to flee from numbers. So he raced down the hall, and heard the yelling of the pursuit fill up the corridor with the thunder of its echoes. He reached the back stairs and hurled himself down to the next hall. There he saw a stream of armed men running up the narrow steps. They sighted him in turn, and bellowed with a sort of angry pleasure that he understood very well. The entire front of the hotel was resounding at the same time. Wolf packs gave tongue all about him, as it were.

He jerked open the first door at his left, slammed and locked it behind him, and saw a bearded fellow leap up from the bed where he had been drowsing.

"Steady, partner, and it'll be all right," said Oliver, and made with his revolver a slight gesture to give point to his words.

The bearded man merely leaned against the wall and laughed. "Coming after you, eh?" he said. "Make yourself at home, Oliver! Half the town can guess that you're Riley Oliver. . . . We all hope you win out, boy! We're doing what we can to help pull the wool over the eyes of Birch and Christy. Go on, man!"

Oliver was already at the window, lifting the sash that allowed a cold river of air to sweep into the room. But the force of the wind swept at an angle across the building, and it was only the backwash of its current that struck against his face with flurries of white. Leaning out, he measured the distance to the ground, which was far enough to promise an ugly fall, except for the heaped drifts of snow that were backed against the wall.

He called to the Masterman, and the great brute leaped onto the window sill, there poised himself, cocking his head to the side to make sure that his owner was giving this strange order. Then, without fear, the dog leaped down into the snow that dashed up in a flying spray from the impact of the heavy body. An instant later he had bounded clear, and Oliver thrust himself through the window. He was hanging by one hand when he heard the door of the room being shaken violently, then dashed in with a splintering crash just as he let go and dropped. His feet struck hard enough through the heaped snow, with a force that snapped back his head like a hammer blow, but he started running without waiting for his wits to clear.

Christy's voice roared above him, rising on a high note of hungry rage, and, as he dodged about the corner of the hotel, a double charge of buckshot whipped the air behind him.

Out of the alley, straight across the street he fled, catching the long leash that dragged behind Masterman. The dog must have tugged it through the hands of whoever held him, when the scent of the master grew close and strong. Otherwise he would have come to the door of Oliver's room with the men of the law hanging onto that strap. That same lead was the very saving of Oliver's life now, as he fled through the sweep of the storm.

He was observed as he entered the street, for a score of men were hurrying toward the uproar in the hotel, and at the cry of some leader they came streaming after him. Speed was what he needed—speed against the shouldering weight of that wind. Masterman gave it to him. A thickening of the snowfall helped him, also, and in five minutes he was free from the immediate pressure.

More trouble lay ahead, to be sure, but he was able to get out of Fairbanks and into the open country. A scant mile from the town, he stopped in the lee of a snowbank that had piled high over a dense growth of brush. That gave him a wall against the freezing hands of the wind, so that he could burrow down under the upper crust of the snow and lie secure in a white dug-out, with Masterman to help keep him warm. It required patience to endure the long misery of that chilly refuge. Several times he had to leave the dug-out and run up and down, beating his arms to restore circulation. And then the time came for his return.

It was near evening when he started for the northwestern

trail, and not far from the long, depressed streak that marked it, he made Masterman dig in under the lee of a white hummock. He would stay there until he was called, curled into a ball, with the fluff of his tail thrown over his nose.

Then Oliver went on toward the lake road. The wind had fallen from its first strength, and now it blew in gusts, with intervals that were almost calm. But the cold had increased greatly. It was more like the beginning than the end of winter.

There was no sight of any man as he drew near the trail. Perhaps Jennings would think it a waste of time to keep the appointment that he had made in such a heat of blood, after learning how Oliver had been hunted out of the town. Eagerly Riley Oliver scanned the hummocks of snow toward the lake, and then toward the town. A great pool of snowdust formed in a whirl of the wind, blotted the town from his eyes, and disappeared.

Then Oliver saw a wide-shouldered fellow running toward him. It was Jennings.

As he came on, he waved Oliver away, and, coming up, he shouted eagerly: "You fool, get back from the trail! Get back, or they'll see you! They'd apt to be traveling the trail in crowds, all day! And all night, too!"

He ran on, with Oliver beside him. They were more like friends than men who were to try for one another's heart's blood in a few minutes.

"What's happened? You mean they're still out in herds, hunting for me?"

"For you? They don't care about you, now. They've got something bigger to think about. Laforge blew out the whole corner of the bank building."

"Laforge? In the middle of day?" said Oliver, wondering. For this very night he was to have met Laforge.

Well, that was no matter to the criminal, if he saw his way

open to get great booty. He would not put it off for such a thing as an interview, of course. Yet the Jap seemed to have attached great importance to the chance of winning Riley Oliver to his cause.

"Right in the middle of Fairbanks . . . in the middle of day," said Jennings, measuring the distance between them and the trail, and then falling to a walk. "Two of 'em walked into the bank, masked. Stuck up the four men in the place and called the cashier for the combination. That fellow had nerve and wouldn't talk, even to save his life. A third member of the Laforge gang came in, and they ran a soap mold around the door of the safe. They were ready to run the soap into the mold, and then something went wrong. They'd come out of the safe room . . . all of them, the lucky devils . . . and while they were out, the nitroglycerin went off with a crash. Maybe it got too cold, or something. It blew the whole corner out of the bank, but it didn't hurt the safe at all.

"Laforge went crazy. He tore the mask off his face. Told 'em his name . . . as though they wouldn't have known his ugly yellow mug anyway. The whole town was coming up on the run. The big gent with Laforge tried to get him away. So did the third fellow. But Laforge stayed long enough to shoot the cashier dead, just as he'd promised. Then he got away, right through the crowd . . . he always gets away, and be damned to him."

Once more Jennings looked over his shoulder toward the trail. He suddenly halted.

"This here looks a good enough place," he said.

"It's all right," agreed Oliver. "Kind of slippery, though."

For the wind had scoured away all the surface snow in this spot, and the under part was almost like clouded ice.

"It's better to slip a little than to have to wade through snow that's like deep mud. Maybe that's what *you'd* like, though . . . with those long legs of yours."

Riley Oliver's powerful body was shielded by no furs. He shrugged his shoulders, now, at the cold and at the words of the smaller man. "This place is as good as another," he answered. "Show me what we fight for, man, and I'm with you."

"We fight for those," said Jennings, and threw a heavy bunch of keys upon the ground.

Chapter Twenty

MAN AGAINST MAN

Oliver looked into the eye of the wind and back into the eye of the man. He tried the hard surface of the snow with a few dancing steps, and found it like oiled glass. However, he was too big to make complaints. Terrain that suited Jennings would have to suit him.

The jailer had thrown off his parka and stood out in a thick, close-fitting sweater. He pulled a Colt from his clothes and dropped the gun on the discarded fur.

"There's my gun, so we can start square," said Jennings.

"There's mine, to make us even," agreed Oliver. And he threw his own weapon beside that of Jennings.

"I've brought two knives," said Jennings. "Take your pick."

He held them by the points of the long, curving blades, and offered them to Oliver. The big fellow took the one that was nearest him and stepped back. They were ready.

Other men had faced one another with nothing but bright steel and with defenseless bodies, but no two men had ever fought together for such prizes—one to gain a desperate chance to set free a friend, and the other to justify and test his own courage in his own eyes.

Jennings began to circle. He kept his head down a little, and canted to one side, as though he intended to use his skull as a shield for his throat, and also seeming to signify his intention of rushing straight in at the first opportunity, and then, at close quarters, stabbing and slashing until one of them fell.

He moved about with his left hand and arm stretched out, as a guard, something after the fashion of a good boxer's posture. There was no doubt that he meant business, and that he knew perfectly how to go about his work.

Oliver's problem was a very different one. He had to win, and he had to win unscathed. A knife wound does not heal quickly, and, if he were hurt, he would have to take shelter somewhere here in Fairbanks until he was fit again. But that was impossible for any length of time. Already he had been found out. If the attention of the town had been diverted from him for a time by Laforge's crime and flight, it would return to search for a less important prey, later on. Everything depended, then, upon his ability to master Jennings while he himself remained unhurt.

So he moved like a great, cautious cat—like a lynx, say, when the winter starvation forces it to engage a full-grown, formidable timber wolf. Carefully feeling the slippery surface beneath him with every step, he moved about the other. The circles in which they passed grew narrower and narrower. They looked like a pair of pugilists, although in this case the very first stroke might well be death.

The big man lunged suddenly. Jennings ducked under the straight thrust, and slashed at the arm. He cut through coat and shirt, and barely grazed the skin. Oliver was carried straight in, skating on the flat of his feet. He jabbed again, for the face—that piece of white, corrugated iron—but again the face bobbed under the driving knife, and Jennings, with a grunt of effort, struck for the heart. A great sway to the side got Oliver out of the way; the knife blade merely sliced through the loose cloth of his coat.

He was still sliding from the efforts of the first lunge that he had made, and, as he went on with an effort, he was able to turn and see that Jennings was no longer the color of stone.

Instead, he was flushed and triumphant, and he danced about on the slippery surface of the snow with perfect ease, as though it had been a boxing mat. His feet, Oliver noticed, scarred the surface; they left little scratches, and bits of white dust flew away in the breeze.

Then Oliver could understand why Jennings had wished to find some such surface as this. Fine spikes on his boots made him perfectly at home, while Oliver careened and glided here and there like a rudderless ship in a high wind.

"I've got you!" said Jennings. "And I've got you good, too. What you done to me, back there in the jail, is what I'm gonna do to you now, Oliver. Holler for help. Get down and beg, like you made me beg! Or I'll cut you up, slow and sure, Oliver! I got you like a fish on dry land." He began to laugh with a horrible violence that wrenched his body this way and that. An insane frenzy of joy and of triumph swept the smaller man in toward Oliver.

Riley Oliver steadied himself. He had that nightmarish feeling of numb helplessness, and the sense that no matter what he strove to do, he was lost. He was like an insect caught in a sticky fluid—like a hawk on the ground, with wings tied together. He could only slip and flounder helplessly, and hope that he might have a chance to strike one vital blow. But he was barely able to turn fast enough to keep his face toward Jennings's darting form. The latter dodged to the side. Oliver strove to change front at once, but his feet shot from under him, and he came slamming down on the flat of his back. His head clicked with stunning force against the ice-hard snow.

But he dared not remain stunned. He had to clear away the black mist that was covering his eyes and see Jennings, coming in like a beast of prey. There was no time to try to sit up and meet the attack. He could only twist his body like a wounded snake and flick out both his feet together.

The legs were struck from beneath Jennings, despite the spiked boots he wore. He reached for Oliver's throat as he fell, and the flash of the long knife went out in a tingling crash of steel, as the blade shivered to bits against the metal hardness of that thawed and re-frozen snow.

Oliver, turning on his side, thrust at Jennings's flank. Jennings, in falling, rolled his body violently, so avoiding the stroke and spinning off to the side. He was on his feet as Oliver regained his. On his feet, and running for the fallen parka beside which the revolvers lay.

Was that the end? It seemed so to Riley Oliver. On that uncertain footing, he could hardly compete with Jennings in speed, and with a revolver at close range Jennings was not the man to miss more than once.

For his own part, Oliver could merely glide forward, skating feebly along, half expecting to fall at every instant, as he saw Jennings reach the guns and stand up again with a Colt in either hand, waving them hysterically and shouting: "Now, Oliver! Now, damn you! Now call me master, or I'll cut you down bit by bit. Drop that knife, and give up."

He might as well have talked to some dumb beast of the woods. Capture meant death to Oliver, and the loss of poor Bob Melville. And as for the girl. . . .

Oliver hurled the heavy Bowie knife straight at Jennings's head. It struck with the flat of the blade across the jailer's face, the handle flicking over against the side of his head. Jennings fired twice with his gun, but the bullets all drove into the snow, throwing up white chunks against Oliver's legs. Jennings himself was still reeling when Oliver reached him.

To strike past the guns was something like putting a hand inside a lion's cage. Instead, he made the knuckles of his left fist bite home against Jennings's cheek bone. He thought for a moment that he had broken his hand; the jar and the pain of the blow shot up into his shoulder.

Yet Jennings did not fall! No, for he stood there with the blood trickling down his cheek, the guns in his hands hanging loosely at his sides, a curious squint in his eyes. Then all at once he collapsed. His knees went first, then his whole body turned to a bag of water and sloshed down to the ground.

Oliver took up the guns first, then the jail keys. He threw both the broken knife and the sound one far away into soft snow. He shivered as they left his hand, for he knew how close that call had been. Over Jennings's brutal face he bowed for a moment. The man was still unconscious. Now the cold of the wind pressed like icy steel against every part of his body. He took up Jennings's parka and forced himself into it. It had fitted very loosely on the jailer; it made a tight but a possible fit on Oliver's huge body.

Jennings sat up, presently, groaning and swaying.

"Get up!" commanded Oliver. "Turn half left. Now march!"

Jennings, without a word, obeyed. In the beginning he stumbled once or twice, so that it seemed he was about to fall. Afterward, he recovered control of himself.

They came to the spot where Masterman was cached. At a word the dog rose out of the snows, like an apparition.

"The wind's fallen, Jennings," said Oliver. "I'm going to leave you out here with the dog. Masterman, guard him!"

The Masterman crouched before Jennings and looked with eager red eyes on the soft throat of the man.

"If you move," said Oliver, "he'll slash your throat. If you try to sit down, he'll tear your heart out. Standing still, maybe you'll freeze. I don't know. But if I can get my job done in time to save you, I'll come back out here and turn you loose."

Jennings regarded him without interest. The blood was

congealing on his cheek. He lifted a hand toward it, but the savage snarl of Masterman, gathering for a leap, stopped him.

"That's the way of it," explained Oliver. "If you lift that hand again, he'll go after you. You see how it is, Jennings. Anything that you can say to help me make that job in jail short will be to your own advantage. If they catch me, you'll freeze to death out here, and nobody will know about it until after the thaw. Going to tell me anything, Jennings, that'll be worth my knowing? Anything that'll help me to get into the jail and out again?"

Jennings regarded him with a bitter calm. "They're gonna know that I gave you the keys," he said.

"Maybe they'll know that," Oliver admitted. "Maybe they'll think that I'm just a wizard. Jennings, what can you say to help me out?"

"I'd rather be damned than help you!"

"You *will* be damned," said Oliver cheerfully. "You'll be frozen first and thawed out in hell afterward. Are you going to talk, Jennings? How can I get into the jail except through the front door?"

"Are you gonna be fool enough to try to get into that jail again?"

"Yes."

"What did Melville ever do for you?" asked Jennings, forgetting his own wretched position, in the depth of his wonder. "Did he save your life a coupla dozen times?"

"He was a friend . . . and we were in hell together," said Oliver.

Jennings considered for a moment, and shook his head. "I stop thinkin' about that. I'm beat," he said. "But there's another way to get into the jail, all right. Try the *back* door!" He grinned sardonically, as he said this.

"How's that guarded?"

"Two men now, day and night. You got through one door, so they're expecting you to come back and try the same sort of a dodge."

"What are they using?"

"Sawed-off, double-barreled shotguns."

Oliver sighed. He passed his hand gently over his body. Riot guns at short distances are no less than murder, and he knew it.

"Yeah, it's kind of mean," said Jennings.

"There's got to be some other way into the jail."

"There's a skylight in the roof."

"What does that open into?"

"It opens into nothing. Sometimes a ladder is shoved up against it when somebody needs to get out on the roof. That's all."

"The skylight's no good, then?"

"Not a bit of good."

"No other way in?"

"Yeah, through the cellar, if you'd like that."

"Tell me about that."

"Well, there's the cellar door, made out of iron and cement. It lies flat flush with the ground, at the southwest corner of the jail. That door's locked. It weighs a hundred and fifty pounds. There's a pair of lanterns lighted over it each day at dark. And there's a man watching the door from the loophole that's sunk in the wall right above it. Besides that, there's another man on guard at the bottom of the steps inside."

"It's impossible," sighed Oliver.

"It sure is," said Jennings.

"And yet I've got to try the cellar. It's the only chance . . . if it *is* a chance."

"It's better than shooting yourself with your own gun. That's all."

"Where do the steps lead? The steps inside the cellar door, I mean."

"They divide at the bottom. One hall goes to the wood cellar. The other hall is shorter. It goes into the cell room where your friend Melville is still kept."

"They didn't move him, then, after I tried that raid?"

"No. That's the safest place in the jail to keep him."

"That hall that goes to the cell room . . . is there a locked door in it?"

"No."

"Who's on guard in the three places, now?"

"Saylor's at the loophole window that looks over the cellar door. Big Bill Day is on guard at the landing under the cellar steps. And Barry's always there in the cell room. Barry stopped you once, and he got a lot of glory out of it. He's ready to die to stop you again."

"All those boys have sawed-off shotguns?"

"Yes. Double-barreled ones."

"My God," whispered Oliver.

"You could put it stronger, too, and you'd still be right," said Jennings. He added, half to himself: "If only I hadn't slipped. If only I'd socked the knife into you . . . damn you."

"I'm leaving you for a while," said Oliver. "So long, Jennings. I know you'd rather wish me good luck than stay here and freeze. Masterman, watch him." He halted to add: "Which are the keys to the cellar door, the cell door of Melville, and to his irons, if there are any on him?"

In silence, Jennings pointed them out, and Oliver strode off toward the town.

Chapter Twenty-One

TO FREEDOM

It was between day and night when Riley Oliver came near the jail. He had made one pause at a hardware store where a fat, sleepy half-breed had waited on him. Now Oliver, with his small purchases wrapped in a bit of canvas, walked straight up to the southwest corner of the jail, unwrapped his canvas, laid it on the ground, and knelt in front of the lock of the cellar door.

"Hey!" yelled a voice through the loophole window nearby.

"Hey what?" answered Oliver loudly.

"Hey, whatcha doin' there, you fool?"

Oliver looked up and screened his eyes with his hand, as though to peer the better at the speaker. The two lanterns were lighted, and hung well out from the wall of the building on brackets, to illumine the cellar door, but the glow they cast could not penetrate the dim half-light of the evening. When the real darkness set in, they would begin to be efficient.

"What d'you mean, what am I doing?" asked Oliver. "Can't you see?" He took a small hammer and tapped at the lock. Then he picked up a screwdriver.

"Look it," said Saylor at the window. "I got a mind to drive a couple loads of buckshot into your hide, you dummy."

"Go and get another mind," said Oliver calmly. "You talk like a half-wit."

"I talk like a what?"

"You heard me, Saylor."

"Hey, who are you?" asked Saylor, apparently amazed

that his name was known.

Oliver went on fiddling at the lock, without making an answer.

"Who sent you out there to fool around that lock?" demanded Saylor. "You talk up, boy, or I'm gonna sock you with some shot, as sure as my name's Saylor. Don't try to get tough around here."

"Listen, Saylor," Oliver said wearily, looking up from his work again. "Would I be here if Jennings hadn't sent me to work on this lock? I ask you, would I be here? Is it any fun for me to be here, workin' at this time of night?"

"Oh, Jennings sent you, did he?" There was uncertainty in the question.

"Well, who d'you think, eh? Think I just came to play around?"

"You're one of these fresh guys, are you?" said Saylor. "I got a mind to go out and sock you on the chin."

"You got a mind, have you? You'll change whatever mind you got, though. It's a cinch to stay inside the house and do a lot of talking."

"Damn it all, I *am* going to come out and bust you one," said Saylor.

His rage brought his voice up to a high whine, but Oliver could trust that the man would not leave his post. In the meantime, he took out the bunch of keys, displayed them with a noisy jingle, and fitted the right one into the lock.

"Who gave you those keys?" asked Saylor in a changed voice.

"Aw, go to Jennings's office and ask," growled Oliver. "Jennings gave 'em to me, of course."

"It beats me," declared Saylor to himself.

The lock turned, and Oliver heaved up the massive pane of the door.

Instantly a ringing voice swelled from the dim pit beneath, down the flight of steps, demanding: "Who's there?"

"That you, Bill?" asked Oliver nonchalantly.

"Yeah, it's me," said Bill.

Through the shadows, Oliver had a glimpse of a powerful man with a sawed-off shotgun in his hands.

"You know this damn' lock has begun to stick, and Jennings sent me around to look it over." He stepped down inside, swinging the door shut above his head. Then he turned to it, and again made play with the screwdriver.

"Wait a minute, son," said Bill.

"I've got to get through with this job. What's the matter?" asked Oliver.

"Who are you? And where'd you get those keys?"

"Aw, I picked 'em up in the street," answered Oliver.

"Trying to string me along?"

"Shut up, will you?" asked Oliver. "I've got something to do here."

"Who are you, anyway?"

"I'm your sister's brother's aunt's husband's nephew," said Oliver. He began to whistle a tune, softly, stopping to grunt, as though a rusted bolt head had hampered him.

"You take things easy, eh?" said Bill the guard. "Listen to me. Far as I know, you might be Oliver."

"Hey! I might be who?" Oliver jerked his head halfway around, but he took care not to move it farther.

"I dunno you from Adam," answered Bill firmly and sternly. "I say, you might be Oliver, for all that I know. Come on down here and tell me about yourself. Look sharp, too."

"Hold on," said Oliver. "You going to make me waste time? Didn't Birch introduce us yesterday? How else would I know your name?"

"I dunno about that. I didn't remember bein' introduced to you."

"Shake your head and get your brains to working," suggested Oliver, again apparently at work on the lock. "My name's Langley. Isn't that easy enough for you to remember?"

"You think you're one of these hard guys, do you?" asked Bill. "Lemme tell you, Mister Langley, I've softened a whole lot of the tough boys in my time."

"Come up here and give me a hand with this damn' lock, and don't yap so much," said Oliver.

"Well, now dog-gone my heart, I *will* come up there," Bill said. "Maybe you think I'm here to be a kind of decoration . . . but I'm not. I'm here to keep an eye around. Come down here! If I have to walk up there, you're gonna wish you'd walked into a half ton of wildcats, instead of me. I'm gonna mend your manners for you, Mister Locksmith . . . or Langley . . . or whoever you are."

"You're old enough to know better than that," observed Oliver.

A sharp oath answered him. A footfall sprang up the stairs, and Oliver, switching about, laid the handle of the screwdriver fairly along Bill's temple. The big fellow bit at the air like a dog, then dropped. His mouth was open, and his eyes were shut. He would not move again for several vital seconds. Oliver almost knew a fear that the man would never move again.

He passed on down the steps to the landing and took the hall toward the cell room. Every instinct made him wish to step softly, but he forced his heels down heavily.

The corridor made a turn; the dull glow of a lantern was straight before him, gleaming on the parallel bars of the steel cell like a reflection in cloudy water. Behind the bars, on the right, was the vague, bulky outline of the prisoner's body. Melville turned his head, and the light glinted on the side of his face.

"Hello, Barry," called Oliver.

The guard was already on his feet, the shotgun in his hand. There would be no bantering with this fellow. His sunken cheeks and his dangerously bright eye showed that he was eternally on his guard.

"Who's there?" asked Barry.

"I've got the keys," said Oliver. "And I'm Riley Oliver."

At that absurdity, Barry actually allowed the shotgun to swing harmlessly aside in one hand. "What kind of bunk is this?" he asked.

Oliver stepped out of the shadows of the corridor with his revolver leveled. "This kind of bunk," he answered. "Put down that gun and stick up your hands, Barry!"

Barry closed his eyes. That mask of weathered bronze above, and of snow white over the jaws, where the beard had once been, and the hard grip of the jaws was doubtless the very nightmare that Barry had been dreaming every hour. Now, as it loomed in actuality before him, he wavered for an instant. Then, groaning, he clutched at the shotgun with both hands.

Oliver shot him down. There was nothing else for it. He aimed low at the hips, and his revolver barked, the immense roar of the shotgun boomed through the room. Thick walls and many locked, massive doors could not keep the sound of that explosive from the rest of the men in the jail, as Oliver knew.

Barry dropped into a squatting position on the floor. The pain of his wound instantly made him straighten out on his back, pawing at the air with his hands like a dog trying to swim in the air, upside down.

Oliver kicked the shotgun out of reach, and with the chosen key unlocked the cell door. Bob Melville said nothing. Not a word of rejoicing. Not a word of thanks. His eyes were gleaming points, already focused on future dangers. His face was set. The third key opened the handcuffs. Melville was free. Free, but inside a jail! And the jail was rousing with a sound of thundering voices, thundering footfalls. Above the deep roars of the men of the law came the high-pitched yammer of the prisoners on the main floor, rejoicing in any mischief that might come.

Oliver pushed a revolver into his friend's hand, gasped to him to follow quickly, and raced down the corridor.

Behind him he heard the door of the cell room being opened, heard Barry screeching that they had gone—"That way! That way! Riley Oliver's here! Oliver! Damn him!"

Big Bill had recovered enough to sit up on the steps where he had lain throughout the vital seconds of the rescue. His face was a blank. He made no move to impede the two men who rushed past him.

Oliver set his shoulder against the ponderous panel of the door and flung it wide. The brilliance of the lantern light, that now seemed to be multiplied by ten, flared strongly down into his face. Across the open, snow-covered ground, he saw forms running toward the uproar of the jail. But as Melville sprang out and the door dropped into place behind Oliver, the bigger man turned not toward these numerous enemies, but toward Saylor's loophole window. He smashed the glass of that aperture with a .45 caliber bullet.

There was a wild howl of fear, astonishment, and pain for answer. Perhaps the bullet itself had clipped the side of Saylor's head. Perhaps it was flying glass that had wounded him. At any rate, his shotgun did not speak a reply, and Oliver ran straight through the approaching men of Fairbanks. A wave of his gun scattered them. They were coming to *look* at trouble, it appeared, and not to take part in it.

Now, with Melville running like an athletic boy at his side, Oliver reached the street and saw the glow of lights before the saloon. All the men inside it—luckily there were only half a dozen—had poured out through the swinging doors. Just beyond was the team of seven dogs and the sled. Oliver's yell roused them while he was still at a distance. That was Budge in the lead—the familiar shout of his master made the big fellow tighten the traces at once. The other dogs struck their collars, and the runners of the sled, only slightly frozen into the ground, came free with a lurch.

A flying start was half the victory, for the men from the jail, hard though they ran, were a good distance behind, and rage cannot lighten the heels like fear.

But here were half a dozen men, well in the path, and every man armed. Revolvers glittered in their hands. Certainly, if they opened fire, they would shoot well and straight.

Then a voice yelled—was it Harlaw the Dane who was shouting?—"It's Riley Oliver, and he's got his partner at last!"

Right past the poised guns fled Oliver and Melville, and not a shot was fired. Instead, an Indian yell of triumphant sympathy came from all those throats; and there in the doorway of the saloon was Harlaw the Dane, leading the cheer.

Melville, sprinting hard, reached the gee-pole; the dogs, at full gallop, raced up the street with a cloud of snowdust shooting up behind the sled.

Chapter Twenty-Two

A MAN'S COUNTRY

Well out of town, they struck the middle of a wild storm that brought the horizon to within a few yards of them, but Oliver found Jennings waiting where he had left him, with the Masterman at his feet. The man was almost a pillar of ice. He turned a dreadful face on Oliver, and went off on staggering, brittle legs toward the town. A swirl of the gale struck him flat. It was minutes before he could get up and go on.

"Will he live through it?" asked Melville.

"I don't care if he lives or dies," said Oliver. Then he put Masterman into harness, and they went on.

They struck across open country, unpursued—at least the pursuit was not in sight—and so they reached the great river running northeast. Still, they were in the white hand of the wind that seemed as limitless as the north out of which it blew. But they were content because of the greatness of the task before them and because, by facing that task together, they could bring the mutual strength of partners. That is a strange chemistry of the mind that makes of the howling wilderness a pleasant home.

Their affection for each other would not have been guessed except by the initiate. On the march they rarely spoke. Often not a word was uttered for hours, the necessary questions being asked and answered through gestures only. Each man knew his task and performed it in silence. As for the dogs, Masterman took care of the teaching and the disciplining of the new Huskies in the team, and it was the turn of his head, or his growl as he pulled, that made the rest of the team behind him bend to their work in spite of the gale that beat and staggered them.

The men had little to do except to drive their own bodies forward, but that was enough. Their faces, blue with congealing cold or flecked with the white of deadly frostbite from time to time, their knees numb with effort, they, nevertheless, kept stolidly at their work. They were men who had endured labor before, and labor to the uttermost. The cheechako cannot stand cold because he thinks of it too much. The old-time sourdough learned to clip the wings of imagination so short that it can never rise from the ground and get at the soul.

When a halt was made, the two fell swiftly to work, for understanding hands waste no effort. The dogs were unharnessed, the wood was cut, the tent put up, the primus stove kindled, food for dog and man was cooked, and all without the necessity of speaking. It was only at the end of the meal, when the last cup of tea was being sipped and pipes were lighted, with the moment to turn in almost at hand, that conversation began. For the most part it was conducted in short sentences. Merely to sit back and look at one another, to revel for an instant in the sense of human nearness in that waste land, was enough—for they were partners by nature.

And on the evening of the first day, they spoke of this matter with concern and with interest, Melville saying suddenly: "That's what makes the life, up here. A chance to know a man."

"There's no chance in a town," agreed Oliver.

"No. You've got to go on a trail together."

"A trail with some red on it."

"Yes," said Melville. "Maybe that's it. You've got to see blood together."

"But down there," said Oliver, with a gesture that indicated the whole southern world, "people live fifty years, and never know one another."

"They talk to one another like print."

"Nothing but words."

"If we come through this, Riley, and ever get south again, one day we'll have to come back."

"We will. After being up here, anything else is like living in a hole in the ground."

"The air's bad, when too many people are around."

"It is."

"And if you know one man, that's enough."

"Yes, if he's a real man."

"And what a man? Brains?"

"A fellow who can spin yarns?"

"No."

"Good nature?"

"No."

Melville puffed for a long moment at his pipe, considering with thoughtful eyes the cloud of smoke that arose, and his own ideas.

"I've been eating my heart out to get back, but now that we're on the last trail, no matter where it leads," he finally said, "I begin to see that a man's country is more to him than his kin."

"Is this your country, Bob?"

"Maybe it is."

"And mine," said Oliver. "I've been thinking it was prison for these nine years. But now I see that freedom to travel doesn't matter so much. A man can never travel outside of himself."

They finished their pipes and turned in. That was the longest talk that they enjoyed together on the trail.

★ ★ ★ ★ ★

On the second day, the wind fell from the weight of a gale to a steady breeze. As they rounded a long bend of the river, the sky milk-white above them with the falling snow, Masterman howled so short a note that it was almost like the bark of a dog.

"Men!" exclaimed Oliver, and waved his hand.

That signal stopped Masterman. Melville, who was ahead, making trail, turned to look back, and saw that Oliver had run from the gee-pole up to the leader. Masterman's nose was buried in the white fluff that covered the ice.

Gently, delicately, Oliver laid aside the feathery snow, and then summoned Melville. They could both see it—the small but clear imprint of a sled-runner on the harder underlying surface. Not many hours ago men had been toiling up the river. The traveler who had left this sign behind him had not passed up the river long before. Some time after the gale had stopped, and before the present snowfall had started, that sled had gone toward the northeast. Very carefully, they cleared more of the trail, bit by bit, until the whole pattern was clear. The marks were very faint, for the packed undersnow was reasonably hard. When the whole picture lay before their eyes, they could see that not one, but two outfits had preceded them.

Melville said bluntly: "These are outfits from Fairbanks, Riley. They've hunted us this far up the trail, and they've overrun us. They're in the snow-fog, somewhere ahead of us. What else but men would anybody be hunting in weather like this?"

"We'll send Masterman ahead to be our eyes and ears," suggested Oliver.

He loosed the Masterman, therefore, and let him range, while they pushed on with Budge in the lead. But in all that time the great dog, that drifted through the snow ahead of them, did not once sweep back like the trained hunter he was to report dangers.

They were tired, when they turned in from the river and camped in the brush behind the bank. Masterman returned to join them, and as usual lay in front of the tent.

It was his snarl, pitched softly as though to convey secret tidings, that brought Oliver suddenly out of the shelter with a rifle in his mittened hands, for he knew the vocabulary of Masterman and could readily turn it into human words. "Danger," said the big wolf dog's snarl. "Danger . . . and men!"

All about the camp, the tops of small bushes bristled like grass above the tops of the hummocks of piled snow, feathery soft as it had fallen. Between a pair of these loomed the form of a man, only his head and shoulders visible. The dogs, at the same instant, broke into a clamor, leaping from their beds and shaking the snow from their flanks with the fury of their barking.

Riley Oliver covered the advancing form with his rifle. "Come on . . . but come slow!" he shouted.

It was a small man who drew near. His hands were raised to the level of his head in token of friendliness. A strange thing it was to see a human being walk in out of the vast Alaskan night in that manner.

"Who's there?" shouted Oliver.

"William Birch," came the unexpected answer.

Melville was out of the tent by this time, with his gun also at the ready.

Birch came to a stumbling halt before them. "I was mushing for Fairbanks," he said. "There ain't anything to be afraid of, strangers. I'm Birch, from the marshal's office in Fairbanks. And. . . ."

"I'm Riley Oliver, and this is Bob Melville," answered Oliver. "Glad it was you who walked in on us, Birch . . . though maybe it's about the last walking you'll do."

"Oliver? Melville?" groaned Birch. "I thought I'd found one bit of luck, at last . . . and instead of that, I've jumped out of the frying pan and into the fire."

"Who's behind you?" asked Oliver.

"Nobody."

"That's a lie."

"I left Fairbanks with two men, but they're up the river, three hours away."

"Why?"

"Shot."

"Shot? Killed?"

"They'll be dead, if I don't get help to 'em. One down with a bullet through his leg. But one of 'em caught through the body."

"Who did it?"

"Laforge!"

"Laforge? He hit the western trail from Fairbanks?"

"He did, and then doubled back and took the river. He nearly give me the slip, back there." He groaned again, as he spoke.

"Come inside," said Oliver suddenly. "Walk inside and make yourself at home. This sounds like something to me." He added: "Bob, go in first."

Melville led the way, and presently all three men were sitting close together on the sleeping bags. Melville, being next to the stove, built up the fire on it, and fed snow into the kettle to make more tea, for it was plain that Willie Birch was badly down. He was blue with cold and continually shuddering. His long nose and chin thrust out from a face that had been withered by great effort. There seemed to be nothing left of him, hardly a spark of his old self. He had been like the Napoléon of a hundred terrible campaigns. But now, even his eyes were dull and lifeless, as he held his big tin cup of tea in both hands, trying to get the warmth from it. In the heat of the tent, he had thrown back the hood, and they saw about his head a bandage, dirty with blood.

So Laforge had won again? Remembering the voice of the man who had spoken to him so calmly in the dark of his room, Oliver could well believe it. Laforge had the quality of steel whose edge will not be turned. Now, it seemed clear, the heart of little Willie Birch had been broken by that steel. The little deputy was burned up to an ash.

"Here's a pipe. Will you smoke?" Melville was asking.

Birch shook his head. He raised the cup to his lips with both hands, and the rim of the tin chattered against his teeth before he drank.

"What happened?"

"I was going to get him, or die tryin'," muttered Birch. "I was never gonna leave the trail, this time, till it was the finish of one of us. And I had two good men along with me. Two good fightin' men that knew how to shoot and didn't fear the devil. We had the best string of dogs that ever stepped, and we closed up on Laforge's trail till it was hot . . . it fair smoked. When we camped this evenin', we laid our bets to get them tomorrow . . . and then they doubled back and got us. Worth was standin' guard. He must have been snowblind or asleep on his feet . . . they shot him through the body. They lay off in the woods and peppered us. First they killed the dogs. Then they got Eddie through the leg. They nicked me and started to rush the camp, but I come to enough to shoot a coupla times." His hand made an instinctive movement toward his head.

"They pulled back into the trees. I heard Laforge laughin'

at us, where I was buried in the snow. He was swearin' he'd given me a final lesson. Then they went off. I patched up Worth with a bandage, and Eddie, too. Eddie can navigate around enough to cut wood and cook. But the dogs are dead . . . everyone of 'em. I started to mush on foot to Fairbanks to send out a rescue party. But I come to the place where your trail turned in from the river . . . and here I am." He tilted back his head and drained the rest of the tea, his scrawny throat working as he swallowed.

"It's the red trail," muttered Oliver to himself, "and it'll be redder still, before the end."

Chapter Twenty-Three

A NEW PARTNER

Melville poured another cup of tea, and began to slice bacon into the frying pan.

"You never could have made it back to Fairbanks," said Oliver. "You're about all in."

"I could have made it back. Because of Eddie and Worth, I had to make it back. My legs would have kept on going till I got there."

"You say there's somebody with Laforge?"

"There's two."

"Who are they?"

"I don't know. They don't matter. Laforge is all that matters. He's gone. Worth . . . he must've gone asleep on his feet. Laforge got us." He stared before him with weary, red-rimmed eyes. "They don't matter," he repeated. "*You* don't matter. None of the little thugs and crooks matter. It's only Laforge. It's the Jap that's the walkin' devil on this here earth."

They watched him intently. Their own troubles had seemed great enough, but they appeared as nothing compared with the agony of this little man with the great soul.

"What made you fasten on him like this?" asked Melville. "Did he ever do anything to you? Is it just because you want to make the law stronger than . . . ?"

"What do I care about the law?" exclaimed Birch. "But Buck Peters was my partner. He took in the Jap and put him up . . . and Laforge murdered him for twenty pounds of dust.

Buck, he was my partner." He frowned, not with pain but an intense concentration as he looked into the past, toward the memory of his dead friend.

"I've heard somebody talk about Buck Peters," suggested Oliver.

The grim caricature that served Willie Birch as a face softened and brightened. "He was a kind of a long, drawn-out drink of water, Buck was," he said. "He was the kind that never said nothin', but he was always there. Old Buck was always there. Well, I'd gone off to freight in some new supplies, and, when I come back, there was the body of Buck bent over the table, frozen stiff. And across the top of the table he'd scratched with the point of his knife . . . 'Laforge.' "

Birch paused, then drained his second cup of the strong tea, boiling hot. He held it empty in his shaking hands, and added: "I been on the trail of Laforge ever since . . . but now he's beat me for the last time. I knew it'd be the last trail I run on for Laforge. And now he's beat me."

Melville found himself attempting to give comfort. "This is nothing. You've got a long record and a pretty bright one, Birch. One man missed . . . that's nothing!"

"I ain't talkin' about a man," answered Birch. "I'm talkin' about Laforge!"

A tin plate heaped with food was placed before him; he looked at it with dull eyes, oblivious to everything but his own thoughts.

"There's always dead men behind him," said Willie Birch. "There ain't a single long trail he's ever run that ain't been red."

The red trail again. The mention of it tore through Riley Oliver's brain. He sat up stiffly and stared at their guest.

"Who's with Laforge?"

"I dunno. Langley the 'breed, for one, I guess . . . judgin' by the way they're movin'."

"Who's Langley?"

"He's the 'breed that can run like a horse all day and all night. He's the fastest trail-man I ever heard of in Alaska."

"D'you notice something here?" asked Oliver.

Birch's dull, red-rimmed eyes turned toward him. The whole soul of the man seemed to be empty.

"I notice that a pair of thugs have got me," said Birch. "But I don't care, Oliver. I knew it was the last trail for me, and the reddest of the lot."

"Notice this," insisted Oliver. "Laforge heads a party of three. We're three. He's got a fast trail-man and a good dog team along with him, but even if he crawled along the bottom of a river, I have a loose leader that could follow him on top of the ice."

"Now what would you be meaning?" asked Birch.

"Our way is down the river. He's ahead of us . . . Laforge. Well, Birch, suppose we managed to run faster than he does? There's nothing I'd like more than to wipe him off the face of the earth."

The proposal stunned Willie Birch.

"The dogs have to sleep," said Oliver. "So do we. Before we start, we'll think it over."

He slid into his sleeping bag and closed his eyes. The last he saw was the cadaverous face of Willie Birch lengthening and shortening as he munched at the food, his eyes as dull and lifeless as ever.

"You want to have him loose?" asked Melville of Oliver softly.

"Why tie him up?" asked Oliver. "Birch is white . . . he understands a white man's ways." And he went into a deep sleep that carried him back to the brown hills of Texas, where white clouds were blowing slowly through the sky. Always, on the horizon of that dream, were the melancholy bells of San Marco. But he seemed to be riding away from them now, and he was not alone on the trail that wavered up and down among the hills.

Oliver slept long and heavily. The other two were already up when he opened his eyes and heard the voice of Birch saying: "He wants to make this run. How d'you stand, Melville?"

"I go where he goes," said Melville.

Then Birch answered: "I dunno that you're in the thing for what you can get out of it, but supposin' we do run down Laforge . . . not that we will, but just supposin'. Nobody would be able to remember that you robbed a bank, Melville, or that Oliver shot a gent nine years ago."

Oliver, as he listened, smiled a little, for it seemed to him pleasant but very foolish daydreaming. *If* they overtook the great Laforge—*if* they beat him down—*if* they lived to tell of the battle—then a safe and happy life might be assured to them, with all of their sins forgiven.

They threw the team into harness, pulled down onto the river, and worked ahead. It was a slow business, for although little snow was falling now, it lay deep above the ice so that they had to break trail through it for the dogs. They could only remember that, if the going was hard for them, it was also hard for Laforge's outfit.

Not far up the river they halted at the spot where Laforge and his men, like three wolves, had rushed onto the camp of Willie Birch. Matters were going well enough there, although Worth was a badly hurt man. There was a bluish tint to his lips, and his eyes were sunk deeply under his brows. He smiled a little, but spoke hardly two words.

The other fellow, tall and gaunt, and bending like a veritable crane over a pair of crutches that he had constructed, was doctoring the wounds of the only two dogs that had escaped death in the attack. He was perfectly cheerful. He said his wound was already closing, and he was sure that he would soon be all right. He would be able to hold out there as if he were in a fort, for a good matter of a month, and all he wished was wings to help them along the trail of Jap Laforge.

Neither tall Eddie nor Worth made the slightest reference to the strangeness of the coming of these two fugitives with Birch. They seemed to take it all for granted. There was only one great necessity in the world, it appeared, and that was the prompt destruction of Laforge.

Oliver and Melville spent two hard hours collecting a vast heap of wood for the wounded men. They needed some tobacco, and they got it. Then the trio departed up the river, with Eddie on top of the bank, shouting at them in a wild voice, and dancing on one leg, as though he were a committee appointed to cheer the departure.

It was harder going every moment. The thaw, which had been halted by the blizzard, had recommenced with the rapid rise in temperature, so that the fluffy upper snow began to quiver in loose masses of moisture. Even hard-packed lower strata were decaying. Two men had to break trail constantly, and one of these was always Oliver, for his strength was like a bottomless well.

They put four miles of this hard labor behind them before they saw smoke rising in a thin, straight column through the windless air.

"It ain't Laforge," said Birch instantly, to put an end to the first hope that had jumped into their minds. "It ain't Laforge. He never would be fool enough to camp that close to us, not even if he thought that all of us was more'n half dead. Melville, you stay here with the dogs, and me and Oliver will go have a look."

They stalked the fire not side by side but from different points of the compass, and it was Oliver who waded through the snow-covered brush until he came in view of the fire—a mere handful of wood. Beside it was a man lying on his side on a bed of twigs, his body curved in to the heat.

For a moment, unheeded, Oliver studied the dark face, deeply worked with lines of pain. Then Birch's voice broke in suddenly from the other side of the man: "What's the matter, Langley? Did they ditch you?"

Oliver looked to see the fellow leap to his feet. Instead, he merely stretched out his hand and dropped another scattering of twigs on the fire. By that it could be known that he was hurt almost to death.

"They ditched me," said Langley.

Oliver and Birch drew close. Agony made Langley's eyes bright; his lips trembled and twitched when he spoke, although he managed to control his voice.

"How come you two throwed in together?" he asked.

"Only by a chance," said Birch. "What happened, Langley?"

"Back there . . . you put a slug through one of us," said Langley. "I'm the one. Right leg, close to the knee."

"Lemme see," said Birch.

"It ain't any good," said Langley, "because the leg's froze, now."

The exquisite and full horror of that face entered the understanding of Oliver little by little. He knew, presently, that the sufferer was dying.

"You're a tough bird, Langley," said Birch. "We could take the leg off . . . if it goes wrong when we thaw it out."

Take the leg off—with a knife and an axe—well, that had been done before, in this northland, and the victim had lived.

"Life's no good with only one leg," said Langley. "Besides, what would you do? They'd as soon hang a one-legged man as not. They's a rope comin' my way, too, if I ever get back amongst folks." He held out his hand. "Gimme a smoke, Willie."

Birch lifted a pipe, placed it between Langley's yellow teeth, and lighted it. A deep groan of relief and contentment came from the lips of the wounded man. He even smiled. His eyes closed, and a sudden relaxation passed visibly through his body. How many hours had he lain there, controlling this torment, waiting for death?

"Besides," said Langley, "your slug ain't the one that done the business."

"What else happened?"

"When the Jap seen that I couldn't keep up on the trail, he got out a Colt and put a bullet through me." He pulled on the pipe, and closed his eyes.

"Wait a minute," commanded Oliver. "You mean that Laforge . . . your own partner . . . Laforge shot you?"

"Well," said Langley, "I'd've weighed 'em down a lot, and they wouldn't want to have me on their hands. They talked together a minute. Then Laforge let me have it."

"And walked off," said Birch, "leavin' you like this?"

"No. I was kickin' around in the snow. He shot me . . . in the stomach." His lip curled as though the mere saying of the thing drove a swifter and more brutal torment through him. "I lay there twistin' around, like a snake that you've stepped on. And Laforge, he laid by, leaned over me, and laughed a good deal. 'It ain't gonna last long, kid,' he said."

"Hates you, Langley? Has he got something ag'in' you?" asked Birch.

"Nope. But he laps it up, when he sees a gent down and kickin'. It pleases him a pretty big lot. Christy wanted to shoot me through the head and put me out of pain. But Laforge wouldn't let him. He thought I'd only last a few minutes."

"Steve Christy?" exclaimed Oliver.

"Yeah, him," answered Langley.

Chapter Twenty-Four

IN FULL FLIGHT

That answer, which was of such importance to Oliver, meant little or nothing to Birch. He said: "Why didn't you take and finish yourself, instead of layin' here like a sick dog?"

"I didn't have no knife, even. Laforge took my knife away from me. I tried to cut my throat, but he kicked the knife out of my fingers."

"Hard luck," said Birch.

"Yeah, hard luck. Laforge is hard," said Langley. "But he's smart, too. He's hard, but he's smart. Only, maybe he wasn't smart to leave me like this. He didn't know I'd live long enough to talk to you. He thought you would give up the trail, Birch. He don't think that you're still drillin' away after him, and he don't know that I'm alive to talk."

Langley smiled at the fire and stretched out his hand toward it with a gesture that cherished the heat. "I thought of building up the fire pretty big," he said, "and then layin' myself in it. But I didn't seem to have no nerve for that. The kind of fire that I could build, it wouldn't be too big. I thought of layin' over and breathin' the flames into my lungs. They say that'll kill you pretty quick. But I didn't seem to have no nerve. The strength kind of dripped out of me, through the hole in my stomach." He shook his head as he considered this marvel.

"Christy . . . ," began Oliver. "What about Christy?"

"Christy? Whatcha wanna know?"

"How does he happen to be with Laforge?"

"They're old friends."

"How old?"

"Away back . . . Laforge worked with Christy on a coupla big jobs in the States. Then Christy went off on his own. He had his stake."

That was the explanation, then, of the small fortune with which Christy had turned up at Travis Junction in Montana, those years before. Stolen money from the first! The thing was so logical, so perfect, and brought his whole conception of Christy to such a head, that Oliver smiled a little.

"When Laforge found that Christy was in Alaska, he called him in. He used him at the bank. That's all. Christy didn't wanna go back to the old line of work, but he was scared to say no to Laforge. Nobody with sense would ever say no to Laforge."

Birch nodded. "Take it slow, Langley," he advised, for the half-breed was beginning to turn a greasy gray by this time.

"Ask me whatcha wanna know. I'll tell you. I'll last long enough to tell you. Only . . . the strength is sort of leakin' out of me."

"Did Christy ever tell Laforge that he robbed the bank at Travis Junction?" broke in Oliver.

Birch waved his hand with an impatient frown at this interruption, but Langley was saying: "Sure. He was proud of that. Even Laforge said it was a slick job."

"You hear that, Birch?" demanded Oliver. "That clears Melville!"

"What do I care about Melville?" said Birch tersely. "Langley, who killed Tucker and Wainwright?"

"Laforge."

"Who killed old man Craven?"

"Laforge."

"Who killed Wesley and young Jimmy Sands?"

"Laforge," said Langley faintly.

"I knew it. I said it. I always said it," muttered Birch. "Who shot Dan Bridgeman through the back?"

Over Langley's ghastly face came a smile; his eyes half-closed in contentment. "I done that myself," he said. "I had a grudge from the old days, when. . . ."

"Never mind that," said Birch. "There's other things that I wanna find out about. Was it Laforge that . . . ?"

He failed to finish the sentence, for the hand that Langley had stretched out above the heat of the little fire had suddenly dropped into the flames—and lay there.

Oliver snatched it out and looked into the glazed eyes of the dead man. "That's all," he said.

"I have no luck!" said Birch. "He could've told me who was the gent that finally got at. . . ."

Oliver looked up suddenly into the face of the man of the law, and Birch broke off his plaint to say: "Nobody deserved it more'n Langley. Nobody but Laforge deserved dyin' this way more than Langley."

"I know," agreed Oliver. "But now he's dead. When the chips are cashed in, the game's ended."

He drew the eyelids down over the lightless eyes, and then stood up. Birch was watching him with a frown.

"I thought you was hard, Oliver," he said. "I didn't know there was this much woman in you. You'll be wanting to dig frozen ground to bury him, the next thing I know. But you'll have to wait for the back trail, Oliver, if there *is* any back trail on this job."

That began the final stage of the trek.

The worst torment is labor in the wet, and it was now wet by day and by night. The weather was constantly warmer. The sky was hedged about by masses of mist, luminous or dull gray, according as the sun struck upon them. Immediately beside them, the sun was always breaking through the vapors and turning the snow to soft mush. They had wet feet that made marching both dangerous and uncomfortable. They had wet sleeping bags that refused to dry out. It was almost impossible to keep even the primus stove working at halting points. And as they strained ahead, growing gaunt and hollow-eyed, only one thing kept them going, and that was the sign left by the fugitives, for it was always fresh before them, the marks of the sled-runners gradually dissolving in the warmth.

The great Laforge could hardly have suspected that pursuit was at his heels. Yet, he seemed urged on as by a whip. It was said that he never traveled in a leisurely fashion, but always as though his life depended upon the time he made. And now he gave further and unwelcome proof of the truth of the saying, for they could close the gap only little by little. Never were they certain of their gains, until on that day when the track turned in to the bank—as it had done before—and did not issue again at a point farther up the stream.

They had gone on a quarter of a mile, half a mile, still waiting for the accustomed trail to issue suddenly, sweeping down the bank and out over the more level going of the river. Then, at last, they realized that the miracle had happened. They had overtaken Jap Laforge. Somewhere, back there in the brush, he was camped with Steve Christy. They had only to go back and head in on the sled tracks in order to find the pair.

They looked at one another, then they made the arrangements quickly. The team would be left at the edge of the river, with Budge to swing it. Masterman, almost as a matter of course, would go in with the three of them—himself as strong a unit as another armed man. Birch could take the lead.

Oliver and Melville would follow him, shoulder to shoulder. So they would come upon a destiny of some sort—for one or for all.

It was the full middle of the day, for apparently Laforge was using the weariness of his dog team as his clock, a thing that other Arctic travelers had done before him. The sun struck up a dazzle from the surface of the snow with little blinding bits of mirrored light where water had collected in the hollows of footprints or in other depressions. The brush had a varnished look, and the snow was falling away from it, leaving little white tufts adhering to the shadowed sides of the stems. It was difficult to go on noiselessly, with that sugary crunching continually underfoot.

They had not yet uncovered anything, when the sudden chorus of the dogs in front betrayed them—a yammering of barks and wolfish howls that seemed to approach, rushing upon them through the low trees and the shrubbery.

"Charge 'em! Charge in!" called Birch over his shoulder, and leaped forward to set the example.

As a matter of fact, Oliver was a stride in front, breaking through the screen on the sight of the small hollow where the dog team had been harnessed to the sleds, and where Christy and the great Laforge were standing with rifles in hand, having been alarmed by the clamor. Oliver, in the lead by a stride or so, pitched headlong over a branch that his foot had caught upon under the soft pulp of snow, and, as he went down, skidding and throwing up a spray like a boat at a launching, the rifles began.

When he got to his knees, he saw that Willie Birch was just getting up from the ground, too, and that he was running forward, his right arm dangling crazily at his side, the revolver clutched in his left hand. Birch fired again and again after the retreating figure of Laforge. For the great Jap Laforge, leaving his partner in the heat of the engagement, was throwing his dog team ahead at a gallop, as he sprinted at the gee-pole, swerving this way and that as the irregularities of the ground threw him out of balance. It was almost as useless to chase him as to chase a galloping horse, but Birch, crippled as he was, went blindly after him.

Oliver saw another affair on the left that needed his attention. Melville, with a wild yell, had forgotten all caution the instant he came from the line of the bushes and spotted big Steve Christy. He charged on him like a madman. A bullet clipped through the flesh along his ribs, another trimmed his left shoulder. Then the rifle jammed. That was the only reason that he was able to get to close quarters. He had emptied a revolver as he charged, hitting nothing but mushy snow and pale sky with the bullets. Now he flung the gun at Christy's head, and dived for him in a good football tackle.

He might as well have hoped to bring down a telephone pole by striking it in the same manner. Christy, with a hand of iron, slugged him behind the ear, then seized the helpless bulk of the stunned man by the hair of the head, and whipped out a hunting knife to finish the fight.

The fist stroke was the first thing that Oliver saw, in rising. The upward flash of the knife was the second. Then a bullet from his revolver struck the body of Christy with an audible impact, like the blow of a hand, and knocked him flat.

Bob Melville remained there, staggering and helpless, his knees bent, his hands outstretched to keep him from falling to the ground.

He was still sick from the blow he had received. Then Oliver reached the spot.

Little Willie Birch, in the distance, had hurled his empty gun with a curse into the deep snow and turned back, holding his broken arm by the elbow.

Chapter Twenty-Five

MANHUNTING DOG

Half-a-dozen seconds had turned the trick. Willie Birch was finished for that trail. Melville was sufficiently crippled to make hard travel impossible. Steve Christy lay dying in the snow. And in the distance the voice of Jap Laforge rang in the wind, faint and small, as he cheered on his flying team. He had escaped, and, once more, at the cost of a companion's life.

It was that which obsessed the mind of Christy, when they propped up his head. He could only whisper the words, and his breath came with a rattle in the chest. There was no use trying to bandage the wound; the instant they saw where the red spot was located on the breast, they knew that the man was done for.

"Think what a fool I've been," said his ghastly voice. "I've had him lying asleep. I could have cut his throat a dozen times. I could have brained him. I could have tied him, and burned him by inches. Instead of that . . . he's gone, and I've played the brave companion, to die and rot for him. Think of it." He stared at Melville. "I would have trimmed you again, Bob," he said. "You're the sort of a fool that I could handle by the gross. But *you* finished me, Oliver. Curse you! The first time I laid eyes on you, I felt you put your teeth on my heart. Something told me that you'd be the death of me."

"There's one sad thing about this, Steve," said Melville. "You're dying, man. Don't you know it?"

"Dying? You lie," said Christy. "A half-hearted fool like you might die from such a thing, but that's not my style. The bullet glanced off the ribs. . . ." He paused, choked by a cough that brought blood to his lips. He wiped his mouth with his hand and saw the red. His eyes bulged in his head. Plainly he understood the meaning of that, for his head dropped back, and his body went limp.

"The money," he said suddenly, opening his eyes, and sitting bolt upright. "The money that I've got in the bank account. . . ."

"Part of it'll go to repay Melville for what he's lost on account of you," said Birch sternly.

"Melville! You mean you think he'll get. . . . Damn him, I'll rise out of the grave. . . ." He actually raised himself a little from the snow, and for an instant his voice came back strong and full. That moment burned out the last of his strength. Like one of those branches that bloom for an instant in the flames of a fire before they turn to a wisp of ashes, so the life flared, and the hatred in Christy's face. Then he went limp, and they knew that he was dead.

"Red," said Birch. "I knew it would be a red trail."

"Laforge and I are left," said Oliver. He half detested the man of the law for putting into spoken words his own exact thought. "Come back to the river with me, Bob. I'll take four dogs and go after him, light and flying."

"You're a fool!" broke in Birch. "Foolish for any man . . . aye, or maybe any two . . . to take after Jap Laforge alone. His brain is longer than your legs."

But Melville, after a glance at the set face of his friend, offered no argument at all.

They went down to the river and quickly prepared the sled. On it they placed a tarpaulin that contained a little parched meal in a bag, some dry kindling, and a few other essentials. That was all, for Oliver would be flying light. He would make two furious marches to overtake the fugitive, then he would give up the trail.

For a team, he took the sled dog, one of the new Huskies that had proved to be an indomitable stayer, Budge, and the Masterman. Only those four—they could outrun most teams with consummate ease, and they would have the iron strength of Riley Oliver to sustain and urge them on. Would that be enough to bring the Jap to bay?

Then Oliver paused an instant to say farewell. "If I get Jap Laforge," he said, "I've probably got a clean bill of health for myself. Understand?"

"If you get Laforge," said the other, laying his hand against his side, where one of his wounds had begun to ache, "you'd be pardoned, even if you had murdered a baby . . . let alone for killing a crooked deputy marshal so long ago that men have forgot about it."

"There's another thing, Bob. If I come back, I'm going to marry Mary."

"If you married anybody else, you'd be a fool," said Melville. "So long, Riley!"

"So long, Bob."

"You blithering idiot," yelled Willie Birch, running to the head of the bank, "come back here! Are you gonna hand-feed yourself to Jap Laforge?"

But Oliver was already running at the gee-pole, with Masterman lining out the dogs behind him in beautiful style. So they swept around the next turn, and disappeared.

"You couldn't stop him . . . not with bullets," said Melville.

The answer that Willie Birch gave was true to his character. "He can't have no luck. God wouldn't let nobody but me get Jap Laforge."

Riley Oliver, far up the river, was straining the team forward. Here, by some freak of the storm, the white snow lay in a shallow film over the well-packed under-surface, and there was no need to break trail. He could run at ease at the gee-pole, while Masterman took charge of the team. The big wolf dog swung them with a human wisdom at the corners, and now and again sent a ripple of apprehensive effort through the line behind him as, without turning his head, he growled a vibrant warning to the laborers.

Hours later, Oliver saw Jap Laforge's outfit before him, and that sight seemed to tell Masterman clearly what was in the air—a race. Next to fighting, he loved racing. From that moment, no man could have maintained the pace that Masterman set with his team. Riley Oliver, clinging to the gee-pole, was hurled forward with vast strides, and, as he ran, he watched the team ahead of him. He had been reasonably sure that Laforge would turn back as soon as he observed that only a single man pursued him. Instead, the man fled like a rabbit before a wolf.

However, that was not entirely strange. Laforge had killed many a man, of course, but he preferred, like a hunting beast, murder by stealth to fair battle. He would run from this danger that trailed him, and only when flight failed would he turn and fight.

So Oliver put his team to full speed, and down the long, easy bends of the river they swept. To the measuring glance of Riley Oliver, it was plain that Laforge was gaining. He had the advantage of numbers on his team, and he himself fled like a wraith beside them.

As for Oliver, he had burned up much strength to make up ground, and he saw that his one great resource was Masterman. To his leader, therefore, he shouted, and Masterman answered with a furious effort. The whole team felt it, and responded with a whining eagerness. They no longer seemed tractable servants, but flung themselves forward, red-eyed and savage as any of their wolfish ancestors in the hunt for meat. The leader was giving tongue before the pack, and the prey was in sight.

They held the sprinting dogs of Jap Laforge even. They gained, by slight degrees, then suddenly demonstrated their superiority and began to walk up on the leaders hand over hand. Twice and again, Oliver saw Laforge look back as the gap narrowed.

It would not be long now. The other dogs were staggering between the traces, but the Masterman rushed on, seeming to bear the entire burden of the sled and the dogs behind him in the fury of his struggle. By their names, Oliver called on the flagging Huskies. But no matter what name was called, the sound fell like a whiplash on the spirit of Masterman and made his mane bristle higher.

They rounded a jutting spit of land behind which the fugitives had been lost to view, for a moment, and it was seen that they had lost ground greatly in the interim. At the gee-pole, the great Laforge had become a trailing figure with head bent down, a creature without force, as though an enormous fatigue suddenly had overcome him. He was there, almost in Oliver's hand—but as the exultation flamed in the brain of the latter, he saw the form at the gee-pole ahead of him waver strangely, like an image made of smoke. Then its legs swayed out to the side in a gust of wind.

Oliver, with a groan of apprehension, understood, and shouted to Masterman. For it was a mere empty dummy that had been fastened to the gee-pole of the other sled! The Jap himself was somewhere along the trail, with a rifle at his shoulder.

The very sound of the bullet was already in the soul of Oliver as he yelled to his leader. Masterman cut suddenly to the left, toward the bank.

Then the rifle spoke. The sound rang in Oliver's brain. A wasp stung him through the flesh beneath the pit of his left arm. He heard the deadly song of the bullet coming down the wind. And now his whole arm was numb. No, for in an instant, the poisonous agony began to throb. Strangely enough, it started not in the actual wound, but in the tips of his fingers.

He had but one arm for fighting. The rifle was useless. There remained to him the Colt. The loss of blood would weaken him soon—and before him was Laforge.

However, as the team shot for a moment in under a steep bank that gave shelter against another rifle shot, Oliver did not hesitate. A blind beast of impulse ruled him utterly. He was like a horse in a cavalry charge, helpless and hopeless, but driven forward by a frantic spirit. He paused to cut Masterman from the harness with a sweep of his knife, and waved the dog before him up the bank and into the shrubbery, following at full speed.

Some element of reason was working in his mind, no doubt, to tell him that whatever was done must be done quickly, before the last of his strength ran out into the hot current that washed his left side. He was clear-minded enough, also, to note that the wind was blowing toward them, and that Masterman had found the scent on it. For the dog plunged ahead, straight through the frozen brush, his head up. Stretched out in a straight line from the tip of his nose to the end of his tail, he looked like a roughly shaped missile that had just been hurled from some gigantic hand. Oliver, with the drawn revolver, followed after.

Through a gap in the brush, he looked out over the bend of the river and saw the team of Laforge going slowly on, at a trot no faster than a brisk walk. Hallucination took hold of his brain, so that the dogs appeared to be running on a river of moving ice—the brush, the snow, the whole landscape was pouring back toward him, to bring Laforge closer.

Before him, a yell clanged sharply to his ear. A rifle exploded. He saw the form of a man spring up, waist high above the tops of the brush—and then the leap of Masterman, the knife-like thrust of the fangs as they struck for the throat, the fall of man and beast together.

Oliver was on the spot instantly. Masterman, close by, was leaping up from the spot where he had tumbled. The man already had regained his knees, the parka ripped away from his throat and breast, and Oliver had another close view of that swarthy skin, that hideous, frog-like face of Jap Laforge.

His rifle had fallen in the snow, but he had snatched out a revolver in that instant of time. It was just clear of his clothes when Oliver's foot kicked it far away, in a winking, spinning arch.

"Back!" cried Oliver.

The Masterman checked his rush by planting his four legs stiffly, and skidding to a halt. The shower of snow that he cast up was flung over Jap Laforge as the man rose to his feet.

If he had a second gun, he made no move to get at it, but he looked from the steady revolver of his enemy to Oliver's face. He himself showed no fear. But while he watched, his eyes were as green as the eyes of a cat.

Not fear, but pride, made him speak his first words. "It wasn't you, Oliver. I had you trimmed and ready to fall. It was the dog. I couldn't count on a manhunting dog, could I?" His voice was filled with irritation. "Just remember that when you herd me back to Fairbanks!"

"I won't herd you back," said the other. "I'm taking you back on the sled, and you'll never feel the bumps, because you're going to travel dead!"

Chapter Twenty-Six

THE RED TRAIL

It amazed Oliver to watch Jap Laforge at that instant, for the smaller man was nodding his head slightly, in the manner of one who understands a hidden motive. All the while his bright, active eyes were working over the features of Riley Oliver. Equally keen, equally bright and sharp and hard, were the eyes of Riley Oliver. So the two stared at one another, and each was plumbed to a greater depth than ever he had been fathomed before.

"You're bleeding, Oliver," said Laforge. "Let me tie the wound up, and then we'll talk."

"We talked once before," said Oliver. "It's no good."

"We talked by night. Men like us . . . we need the daylight. Words are only half the talk that goes on between people like us."

"What would you have to say?" asked Oliver curiously.

"The same things as I said the other night . . . only, much more. Because I only partly knew you then, and now I begin to see the whole picture of Riley Oliver." He said it seriously, adding: "You know, Oliver, they want you . . . they have a rope waiting for you. But if you worked with me, you could open the whole North. You could open the safe that holds its jewels and gold. We could make enough money to buy a pair of kingdoms in the South Seas, and go there and live as men like us really ought to live."

"Look, Laforge," answered Oliver, "I've been on your trail only a little way, but it's been dripping red all the time, and your enemies aren't the only ones that go down."

"Well?" challenged Laforge.

Greater than the loathing and the horror that he felt for this man, a vast curiosity sprang up in Oliver. How would Laforge attempt to justify himself?

"A fellow who's worked a hundred trails with you, and saved your scalp twenty times by what he could get out of a dog team . . . the moment he's wounded, you put a bullet through him. I saw him die, back there. We got there in time to hear him talk a little."

"Did you?" asked Laforge. "Half-breeds are always tough. When you cross the blood, you thicken the skin, it seems. So he lived that long?"

"Yes. He said enough to clear Melville, and Birch was witness."

"I'm not sorry about that. I had nothing against Melville."

"What did you have against that poor devil you pistoled?"

"Nothing in the world. As long as he was on his feet, he was worth more than any other man to me."

"But when he was wounded while he fought for you?"

"Then he was a weak spot. He was a burden on my hands. Of course, I put him out of the way. A fellow like that," added Laforge, "is not to be considered on an even basis."

"There was Steve Christy," went on Oliver. "Was Steve beneath considering, too? You ran and left him to take the medicine that was ready in the bottle for you to swallow."

"He was a traitor," answered Laforge.

"Ah, you don't like traitors, Jap?"

"No. Christy betrayed Melville. He'd betrayed others. He would have double-crossed me at the first chance. So I let him have his own medicine. That was all."

"But still you try to persuade me that you'd work on the level with me?"

"You ought to be able to see that for yourself. You have a brain. And you're straight."

"So you'd make a partner of me, eh?"

"Not a full partner. One-third to you . . . and two-thirds to me, the first year. After that, as you worked into my methods, we'd make an equal split of everything."

Oliver smiled faintly and pressed his left arm closer to stop the bleeding. "And I'd be fool enough to trust you?"

"You'd be a fool not to trust me, Oliver. You're the only man I've ever met in my life who gave me odds and beat me. I hate your heart for beating me . . . but I'm too wise not to see that I could use you to the limit. If we teamed together, who could beat us?"

Who, indeed! Oliver had been able to live for nine years outside the law. If he teamed with Laforge, who would be able to handle them? They would roam the Northland like a pair of wide-winged eagles, ruling the country. For one instant, the temptation worked cruelly in Oliver's heart. Then he drew a sharp breath that sent a pain, twisting like a snake of fire, through the flesh of his left side.

"There's your Colt, yonder," he said.

"You're going to turn your back on a fortune, Oliver?"

"That's it. Get the gun, Jap."

"All right," said Laforge. Yet he shook his head and actually sighed. "I hate to do it," he declared. "You want to give me a fair chance, and an even break. It proves what I was saying . . . that something in our blood speaks to one another."

"The blood that's the same in us is what I want to get rid of," answered Oliver. "Are you ready?"

The Masterman crouched nearby, growled horribly as he saw Laforge pick up the fallen weapon. He glanced with a red-stained eye at his master, but, receiving no order, he remained ready to spring, in slavering readiness for the kill. From his position, he appeared to be the judge between the two in this duel that was about to take place. The dog was still panting, and the mist of his breathing divided in the soft wind, blowing back on either side of his shoulders.

Laforge turned to Oliver, the gun hanging from his hand. Oliver, in exactly the same way, faced him.

"Are you ready, Oliver?"

"Ready. Make your move."

"I'm going to kill you, but it's because you're forcing me to. I'm armed and equal with you now, Oliver. For the last time, will you think over what I say? Because it makes me sick at heart, man, to think of throwing you away like this, making dog food of you."

To Oliver's bewilderment he found nothing but perfect sincerity in the voice of the other, a ringing honesty, a burst of emotion that came straight from the heart. There was no doubting it. There was, in fact, something between them—blood of the same nature, a mind that moved on the same springs.

"I'm ready," said Oliver. "And I'm half sorry, Jap. It's like closing the door on some grand things that we could do together . . . but here's the end of this trail . . . for both of us, maybe."

"Well, we'll get it over . . . and God help you!" said Laforge fervently. "We'll count to three. . . ."

They counted to three. The act flung Oliver back to the days of his boyhood—to his schooldays, when a class counted in unison. He saw the hardening of Jap Laforge's eyes; he felt his own strange sympathy for the man dying.

"Three!" And they fired together.

Each moved at the last count. Jap Laforge stepped aside as lightly as a dancer. Oliver, with more wisdom, merely jerked down his head, and, as he fired, he heard the whine of the other bullet beside his ear. He had known with a sure instinct that Laforge would shoot only for the head. He had understood it by his own impulse. He had not missed. He thought that it might be only a glancing shot that had spun Laforge around and dropped him to his knees. But, when he stepped up, he saw the frightful wound in the man's forehead.

Jap Laforge was dead at that instant, although he was still kneeling. It was impossible that he should be alive, and yet his lips were speaking: "I'm almost glad I. . . ."

That was all. With the sentence unfinished, Laforge slumped forward, and Oliver caught him by the shoulder. But only a loose weight sagged down from his hand. He could not save Laforge from that fall, for he had already dropped from this life.

Long after, through the dusk that served as night, Oliver brought the two dog teams back to the camp. Melville and Birch came to him, running, shouting. They caught at him. They howled questions. They gesticulated.

He beat them aside and stretched himself by the fire, for his brain was sick and giddy, partly from the loss of blood, and partly from a thought that been working in him. Still he could hear the others shouting. They were close by, but they seemed to be in the vast distance. They had found the body that was lashed on the rear of the sled, and no doubt they were rejoicing over it.

Afterward they came back and replaced the clumsy bandage with which he had tied up his wound. They spoke to one another freely about him, as though he were a child unable to understand the words.

"He's gonna be a free man," said Willie Birch, "but that don't matter to him. You'd think that he'd killed his brother.

You'd think he'd left some of his own blood back there at the end of the trail."

"Build up the fire, Birch," said Melville. "We'll get him to talking about it, after a while, and that will take the weight off his mind."

Chapter Twenty-Seven

THAT FINAL DAY . . .

Perhaps talk was what Riley Oliver needed, but they got nothing from him that night—nor the next day, when the wounded men started on the snow trek back to Fairbanks. Not even when they had picked up the wounded at the first camp and gone on, nor when they had arrived at Fairbanks with the dead man.

Oliver was under arrest now, and he was being held for the murder of a deputy federal marshal, nine years before. But the people of Fairbanks lodged him in a hotel and not in the jail. The officers of the law concurred in this treatment.

The leading citizens of the town appointed a committee that called on the invalid and offered him a handsome purse, only to have it refused.

"You can do one thing for me," said Oliver. "Give Jap Laforge a decent burial, even if you don't put him in consecrated ground."

They consulted grimly. No other man in the world could have gained their consent to such a thing, but they could not refuse Riley Oliver.

So the frozen ground was trenched, and all of Fairbanks came to the funeral, where Willie Birch made the burial speech in a whimsical style. He said that the best-known man in Alaska was being put underground that day. He pointed out that for courage, brains, and fast traveling, no one had been the equal of Jap Laforge. He was a self-made man who had risen to the top of his profession. He was an independent spirit who had lived as free as a hawk. And finally, now that

Laforge was dead, he—Willie Birch—was without an occupation.

"All these years, he's been breaking trail for me," said Willie Birch, "and now I'm gonna miss him a lot."

The people laughed not a little at the speech of Willie Birch, but Riley Oliver did not laugh at all. He seemed to have lapsed into a long dream.

The last day is still dear to all the citizens who remember it, or even those who have merely heard the tale. It is one of those things that men like to take to heart and tell and retell, gaining a new taste with every repetition.

The days of waiting had been long, to the joy of the hotelkeeper, for as long as Oliver was under his roof, the hotel was packed and the restaurant was always filled with the curious who sought a glimpse of the hero.

There was always much to talk about. For instance, there was the day when Willie Birch, with his arm in a cast and the cast supported by a sling that passed around his neck, came to call on Riley Oliver. The big man and the small man sat at one table, and Oliver cut the meat for the one-handed man of the law, and the whole packed roomful grinned with delight to see the lion and the tiger lying down together, as it were.

Then there was the occasion when two reporters tried to get to Riley Oliver, only to be detected when they were halfway up the stairs. They were plucked down again, and kicked into the street, and then kicked down that street with enormous gusto. For Riley Oliver had announced that he did not wish to be annoyed.

Fairbanks had made him her hero. That he still lived under the shadow of the law made his figure only the more attractive. It was the season, moreover, when men were feeling the release from winter. The ice had broken up in the great rivers and gone out. The snow had melted from the ground in every exposed place, and all the thews and sinews of the heart were at ease. The brief summer would soon be there, surrounding them all.

Now came the final day.

One of those same reporters, who had been kicked down the street by Riley Oliver's indignant friends, now presented himself at the door of the hotel, and managed to get as far as the desk. To the clerk he bent over and whispered a few words, and the clerk leaped up and was seen to turn pale. He caught the reporter by the shoulder.

"Miss Melville has to know," he said.

"Bad news!" muttered the crowd, as it overheard this exchange. And they flooded after, soft-footed, filling the stairs, filling the halls, gathering in scores of people from the street, attracted by the insidious attraction of "news."

Miss Melville was not in her room. She was sitting with her father, who, stretched in bed, was dictating letters. His wounds had been more serious than those of the rest. She came to the door to face the intruders, and the reporter leaped closer to whisper three words near her ear.

She gave a cry that brought her father half out of bed. Down the hall she went at full speed, a channel opening with magic quickness at her coming, through the living press. She reached the door of Riley Oliver's room. At her knock, Willie Birch's voice shouted: "Who's there? Get out!"

For Willie Birch spent most of his days, now, keeping guard over the prisoner.

"It's I!" called the girl.

A terrible growl answered her.

"Hey, wait!" said Birch. He pulled the door open suddenly, and out Masterman leaped, hurling his terrible bulk at the girl.

This the reporter, shrinking behind her, fully noted, and turned green with fear. Then he saw the girl put an arm around the shaggy throat of the wolf dog.

"What's the matter?" called Birch.

She held out her free hand to Oliver. "Riley!" she called.

That famous man was resting on his bed, against heaped-up pillows. No one who has ever been a cowpuncher enjoys leisure in a chair! Now he lurched to his feet and came with enormous strides.

She managed to get past Masterman and meet Oliver in the middle of the room.

"What's the matter?" he repeated.

She held up both arms to him.

"Damn bad taste!" said the reporter, recovering from his fright and shaking his head a little. That would certainly have to go into his newspaper account of this moment.

Moreover, Riley Oliver seemed not in the least embarrassed by this moment. He simply picked her up in his embrace, and at the same time she cried so that everyone in the hall could hear it: "The news has just come! The governor has wired that you receive a free pardon . . . a free pardon! It's a long wire, but that's the gist of it."

At this, such a cheer went up that the ears of the reporter were almost deafened. A man in a bathrobe brushed past him and entered the room. That was big Bob Melville, with a face crimsoned by excitement.

The reporter tried to follow, his notebook in his hand, but several brawny hands grabbed him and plucked him roughly back.

"That's a *family* party, boy," said one man.

"Birch doesn't belong in there, then," shouted the reporter.

"He belongs by adoption," said one of the sourdoughs.

A chunky fellow came shouldering his way through, grasped the knob of the door, and tore it open.

"Hey, there goes another!" yelled the reporter. "How does he get in?"

"Who could keep him out?" roared a burly miner. "That's Harlaw the Dane!"

About the Author

Max Brand is the best-known pen name of Frederick Faust, creator of Dr. Kildare, Destry, and many other fictional characters popular with readers and viewers worldwide. Faust wrote for a variety of audiences in many genres. His enormous output, totaling approximately thirty million words or the equivalent of 530 ordinary books, covered nearly every field: crime, fantasy, historical romance, espionage, Westerns, science fiction, adventure, animal stories, love, war, and fashionable society, big business and big medicine. Eighty motion pictures have been based on his work along with many radio and television programs. For good measure he also published four volumes of poetry. Perhaps no other author has reached more people in more different ways.

Born in Seattle in 1892, orphaned early, Faust grew up in the rural San Joaquin Valley of California. At Berkeley he became a student rebel and one-man literary movement, contributing prodigiously to all campus publications. Denied a degree because of unconventional conduct, he embarked on a series of adventures culminating in New York City where, after a period of near starvation, he received simultaneous recognition as a serious poet and successful author of fiction. Later, he traveled widely, making his home in New York, then in Florence, and finally in Los Angeles.

Once the United States entered the Second World War, Faust abandoned his lucrative writing career and his work as a screenwriter to serve as a war correspondent with the infantry in Italy, despite his fifty-one years and a bad heart. He was killed during a night attack on a hilltop village held by the German army. New books based on magazine serials or unpublished manuscripts or restored versions continue to appear so that, alive or dead, he has averaged a new book every four months for seventy-five years. Beyond this, some work by him is newly reprinted every week of every year in one or another format somewhere in the world. A great deal more about this author and his work can be found in *THE MAX BRAND COMPANION* (Greenwood Press, 1997) edited by Jon Tuska and Vicki Piekarski. His next **Five Star Western** will be *THE OUTLAW REDEEMER: A WESTERN DUO*.